Shadow Outlines

By Munya Chaparadza

Dean Thompson Publishing

Copyright © Munya Chaparadza 2022 of Trof Publications

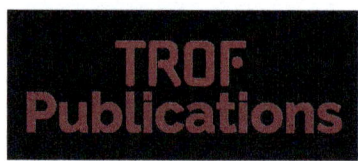

The right of Munya Chaparadza to be identified as the author of Shadow Outlines has been asserted by her in accordance with *The Copyright, Designs and Patents Act 1988*.

Without limiting the rights under the copyright reserved above, no part of this publication may be reproduced, stored in, or introduced into a retrieval system, or transmitted in any form or by any means (electronic, mechanical, photocopying, recording, or otherwise) without prior written permission.

ISBN: 9798410604390

Contact Munya
Telephone: +44 7985 631610
Email: munya@trofpublishing.com

To my children, Tinotenda Reece Chaparadza and Shona-Marie Chaparadza, this book is dedicated to you. I want it to be proof that you can set out to be anything you want to be in this world. Life is tough, but hard work, self-belief and tenacity will get you everything you need.

Acknowledgements

I would like to thank my family, friends and my loved ones.

About Munya

Munya Chaparadza is an entrepreneur, content creator and a brand ambassador for a leading technology firm. Born in Zimbabwe, he moved to the United Kingdom two decades ago. He now resides in Derby, a beautiful city which lies along the River Derwent. Munya considers his family most important to him. If he is not spending time with his family, you can almost always find him creating pieces for his clothing line and promoting comedy shows. *Shadow Outlines* is Munya's first fictional novel.

Chapters

Chapter 1 – Mozambican Scat   1
Chapter 2 – Hymns and Verses   5
Chapter 3 – Leicester City   8
Chapter 4 – In All Her Glory   21
Chapter 5 – Simukah Gorah   30
Chapter 6 – Mr Dean   33
Chapter 7 – Vasco Da Gama   41
Chapter 8 – Will You Mary Me   49
Chapter 9 – Meet The In-Laws   61
Chapter 10 – Vacheron Constantin   71
Chapter 11 – Trust Nobody   79
Chapter 12 – Lost Ones   95
Chapter 13 – Gut Feels   102
Chapter 14 – Horombo   121
Chapter 15 – Avalanche of Fear   133
Chapter 16 – Right Under My Nose   143
Chapter 17 – Penance   168
Chapter 18 – 7 Hotoft Road   184
Chapter 19 – Coalville   198
Chapter 20 – Blood Thirst   203

CHAPTER 1
Mozambican Scat

"We can't just let her burn in that house. Please! Let's go back and get her," she screamed and cried out. Her mouth was still bloody and so were her clothes. She was crying so hard that she could barely get her words out. Death had never been so near and she believed she had come face to face with the devil. Everyone else in the car was completely shell-shocked. It was impossible to believe they made it out. They drove out of the vicinity unsure of where they were headed. One thing was for certain, the city was no longer safe for them to live in, better yet the country itself.

Reggie was born Reginald Pereira Jr., a child of two African immigrants who had fled the civil unrest in their native country of Zimbabwe. His father, Reginald Pereira Sr., was a white Portuguese settler who married a Black Mozambican woman. Mozambique is a small country located in the South East coast of Africa and it gained its independence in 1975 after at least about 470 years of Portuguese colonial rule. During the years between 1974 and 1975, many men and women had to pack up and leave the country due to many so-called terrorist activities that took place. The most publicised ones being the alleged molestations and rape of women at various roadblocks set around the country as the minority whites orchestrated their intricate exit from the new nation. Many of these people had close ties with South Africa and Rhodesia, which is modern day Zimbabwe. Both countries absorbed about 120 000 Mozambicans after the October massacres of 1975.

Reggie Sr and his wife Kainga settled in their new home in a small suburb located a few miles away north of the Capital city – then Salisbury, now called Harare. They lived there for many years and life for them was much richer and somewhat fulfilling. Kainga worked as a nurse at the local hospital while her husband opened his own antique store in the city. It was the first of its kind back then, so unsurprisingly it was a very successful enterprise.

In December 1979, the couple gave birth to a son and they named him Reginald after his father.

Two years later, they had a daughter whom they named Esther. They had a middle class upbringing, which at that time meant having a serene suburban life.

As a child, Reggie was a lanky kid with a long face, brown expressive eyes which always spoke volumes. Typical of most biracial kids from that era, he had a long fuzzy Afro, which matched his brown skin with warm orange-red undertones. In contrast, Esther's skin was more fawn and freckled. She was a little chubby as a child, but they had similar hair which really made them stand out. Their father was an alpha male who raised his family in a patriarchal way deeply rooted in the way his father raised him.

His son was more fascinated by technology, cars, computers and software programming. It was a passion he had since his mother bought him his first game console – the Sega Genesis mega drive – on his 16th birthday back in 1995. He had posters of most action movie heroes from that era, little action men toys and cars. His favourite game was 'Warlock' in which the main character was a druid who set out looking for Titan Runestones before the Titular Warlock used them to take over the world.

Reggie was so hooked to this game that he had no problem staying in his room all day firing bolts of magic at his enemies. All you would hear when you walked past his room was the unrefined audio crackle from the console, similar to that you get from an old set of speakers.

Reggie's room had a small bed which was always neatly made because his mother was strict when it came to keeping the house tidy. He had two straight-backed chairs, which were in front of a Westbury Grey table with three drawers. Unsurprisingly, their house always had old furniture, which he and his sister, with their infant minds, always associated with the horror movie Child's Play. Directed by Tim Hollands, it featured the freaky doll Chucky.

Though the movie was released in the late 80's, it was still popular in the 90's. Their father had got them to watch it one evening on VHS cassette. Some of the scenes had creepy home décor reminiscent of the furniture at their father's store and in their home. This was the main reason why they rarely went to the store. Their dad spent a lot of time in the store basement. No one was allowed to go down there and he kept the door locked.

CHAPTER 2
Hymns and Verses

Kainga was a well-respected member of the local Baptist church and she had a lot of responsibilities. She organised many events at the church. Every Sunday Reggie and Esther would wake up early, have breakfast, get ready and head out to church with their mother. They had been doing this as far as they could remember. They grew accustomed to the elaborate outfits, tambourines and the sight of women constantly adjusting the position of their itchy pantyhose.

Back then, church on Sunday took all day and kids would be separated from adults to stop them from disrupting the sermon. They would dress up in their best clothes and show off to each other. Bible stories and lessons were taught in a playful, fun manner, so for the most part church was fun.

For their mother, church was a domain for self-expression and the pursuit of self-identity. Being around people who displayed courage and strength, gave her hope and belief that her own life would get better. Church was a sanctuary and she felt safe away from the abusive hands of the father of her children. They used to attend church together, but then he stopped going.

When people asked her why he was not attending anymore, she always had the perfect excuse. Kainga would tell church members that her husband was busy working at the store, doing home improvements or away on a trip, buying furniture. Many knew her husband as this charming, kind, charismatic man who was always nice to people. In fact, whenever there was anyone in the church who needed a helping hand or some financial assistance, he would always offer to help. This made him well liked in the community.

In public, he was a nice guy, but behind closed doors he was a totally different man. He was very well calculated with his abuse towards her. She started doubting her own reasoning and actually believing that she deserved the physical and emotional abuse. The situation was worsened by the fact that she was away from her family. It was difficult to confide in anyone, especially the church community who had a gloomy outlook on separation and divorce in general. Afraid of being judged, ashamed or being labelled as an example of a derailed marriage, Kainga buried her abuse in bible verses and hymns.

She would close her eyes while singing songs. The words would induce her into a state of consciousness, becoming highly responsive to the lyrics in a trance like state. Often, she would get completely absorbed in the singing and it would feel as if her soul had wings. The angelic wings would raise her soul from her body and swiftly levitate to the silver zinc church ceilings giving a feeling of freedom and enlightenment. As the congregation transcended in synchronised harmony, the awe and wonder took the weight off her shoulders and she was addicted to that.

Sometimes she would find herself trying to recreate this feeling at home. Bible in hand especially after an altercation with her husband, but it wouldn't happen. The fact that she could not regale the church atmosphere often left her feeling more frustrated than the actual fights. Despite everything, Kainga still loved her husband dearly so she held on and hoped for the best.

CHAPTER 3
Leicester City

The music was loud, but the numerous conversations from the people standing and some sitting around the poseur tables drowned the Neptune produced song by Justin Timberlake. "Rock your body", played from the high-end sound system. The dramatic rubato of the song was the perfect soundtrack for Thursday evenings at the Crypt. It was a swanky bar nestled in the heart of Leicester city centre in the United Kingdom.

Reggie was threading his way through the crowd, scanning around to see where the people he was looking for were located. He would occasionally stop and talk to people he recognised or had hung out with, before continuing to meander his way through. At six foot four, he was very noticeable especially in his white button-down shirt, which was tight fitting and extenuated the lines of his chiselled physique. He had not gone home to change into more relaxed attire. Instead, he just took off his tie and jacket. He unbuttoned the first three buttons on his shirt to give him a less formal look. It would have been impossible to miss the way some of the women he was brushing past were looking at him with lusting eyes and inviting smiles.

Reggie paid less attention to this as his eyes carried on darting around searching for his friends.

"Damn, I should have gone home to change because at this rate my shirt is going to be stained" he said to himself.

He cut across the warm bodies around him rubbing shoulders and trying to avoid drinks being spilt on him. Sometimes the way the place would get packed made him contemplate picking another hangout spot. When it got busy, trying to avoid drinks being spilt on you was like trying to avoid sand at the beach. At that moment, he heard a familiar voice call out his name.

"Reggie, Reggie over here man!" he looked towards the bar were Chris was standing under one of the many grand vintage chandeliers.

They provided perfect dim lighting to complement the 1920 inspired décor of the place. The oversized paintings of Renaissance nudes added to the aura of pure decadence , which was one of the main reasons the Crypt was their favourite hangout.

Rumour had it that a local, wealthy couple owned it. Located on the corner of St Nicholas place and the high street, it was the ideal location for the city's elite. Football players, lawyers and even some government officials liked to hang out there. It was only a short walk from the train station. This made it ideal for high fliers who frequented the city.

The opulent Romanesque-styled building with imposing stone walls, made it almost intimidating for the average person to walk in. Reggie and his friends liked that because it made them feel like members of society's high echelon.

"What took you so long man?" Chris asked in a husky voice, trying to conceal his excitement from the two ladies he was standing with.

"Sorry man, I had a last minute workload which needed my immediate attention; sorry to keep you guys waiting," Reggie said while slapping his hands with Chris's in greeting.

"I told you they're working you too damn much at that job man. They need to give you a raise or you can come and work with me," Chris said with his left hand holding a glass of VSOP, D'usse to be precise.

He wore a black Ralph Lauren shirt with the sleeves rolled up below the elbows revealing a bi-metal Vacheron Constantin automatic Swiss watch.

A keen collector of watches, Chris always had on a different wristwatch to match the occasion. Everything about Chris from his mannerisms to his attire choice, showed that he had a wealthy upbringing. He would use this to his advantage especially in approaching and entertaining women. Apart from that, he was quite an average looking guy who could be socially awkward at times. Reggie was surprised

Chris had managed to keep the two ladies occupied for that long. They were definitely polar opposites, but their personalities positively contributed to the friendship.

"Ladies, my apologies for being late. I'm Reggie and you are?" He asked, lifting the glass of Cognac Chris had ordered for him to his lips to take a sip.

He tried not to react to the usual first burn on the tongue and throat you get from that first sip. His attention was entirely fixated on the two beautiful ladies who stood before him.

"I'm Carmen," she said in a sultry silky voice.

"Nice to meet you Carmen."

"Hi Reggie and I'm Freya", she said in an equally tantalizing voice.

This had him feeling like he was being made to pick one from two of his favourite destinations - Vegas or Miami.

Both Carmen and Freya were very attractive ladies. He kept his cool.

"Lovely to meet you Freya" he said before taking another sip of his cognac, this time swallowing a lot more to trying to come back to his senses.

They carried on with the small talk for a little while and he found himself drawn to Carmen. She had mentioned that she travelled to Portugal on several occasions , which happened to be his heritage.

When he told her that he spoke Portuguese, it immediately made them click. He noticed that she had beautiful spellbinding brown eyes , which complemented her smooth brown skin. The waiter came and told them that their table was ready. Like true gentlemen, Chris and Reggie gestured the ladies to walk in front of them towards the sitting area of the bar where both food and drinks were served.

Freya led in front followed by Carmen who moved in effortless saunter past the see-through shelves where the lighting was a little brighter. It extenuated her amazing figure.

Both ladies wore high heels, but Reggie was drawn to Carmen's black ankle straps. They really complemented her outfit and exaggerated the swing in her voluptuous hips. He remembered the words of the famous designer, Manolo Blahnik, which he had read in one of those fashion magazines they always have laying around at the doctors waiting room—"People walk differently in high heels; your body sways to a different kind of tempo." She was definitely beautiful in the classical way.

"Hi! This is Reggie Pereira from Pegasus Properties. I got the message you left with my assistant. Are you still looking to buy a home?" he paused listening to the response from the voice on the other end of the phone.

"Awesome, now let me ask you before we even get started. Have you already signed on with an agent already? ... Well that's perfect Mr Dean we are on the right track and if you don't mind me asking, are you going to get a bank loan for this property or is going to be a cash purchase?"

The client on the phone wanted to purchase a new home with cash, which was excellent news for Reggie.

However, as a licensed agent, there were procedures they needed to go through first. He always gave clients time to figure out the budget they had and the cost of properties they wanted. He would then put together a portfolio of properties to show the customers also giving himself, the client and properties, enough time to get ready for viewings.

Reggie had mastered the art of dealing with high-end potential buyers. When he dealt with these types of clients, timing and preparation were of utmost importance. He knew clients would go to another real estate company if they sensed any type of incompetence.

During the phone conversation, he found out that Mr Dean and his wife were retired professionals looking to downsize. Their ideal property would have to be specific to their needs. Reggie scheduled for them to come into the office and go through a mandatory questionnaire which would help to establish the exact requirements.

Pegasus Properties were one of the first companies to use state of the art computer software to generate suitable properties for the clients. It would yield results from a database with real estate properties in ideal areas and email them out to the client.

This gave Pegasus Properties an extra edge over the other companies mainly because clients had the opportunity to have a head start by driving around the neighbourhoods of suggested properties by themselves first. Their mantra at Pegasus was buying a home is not a process of selection, but a process of elimination. This was a typical conversation for the top-selling agent at Pegasus Properties where he had worked his way up for the past five years. After setting up a buyer consultation agreement appointment with Mr and Mrs Dean on Wednesday at 3pm he finished the call and asked his assistant to schedule in the appointment for him as a reminder.

When he left school, he joined the army cadets which were exciting, full of adventure and exhilarating. He undertook army proficiency training which taught leadership skills, discipline and self-confidence. He transformed himself from the skinny lanky kid he was, into a muscular more organised young man. Like his dad, he had grown a lot taller and as required by the cadets he had trimmed off his trademark afro and now had short well-groomed hair. He was a handsome looking young man, so it was no surprise that he was a hit with the ladies.

Reggie and his friends used to sneak out to meet girls, smoke weed and drink alcohol. He found this to be a lot more exciting than the actual cadets calling, which he had really joined to fulfil his father's wishes. Eventually, he got kicked out for constantly breaking the rules. Several dead end jobs followed, from doing general warehouse work, construction and being a bouncer in local clubs.

During his time as a bouncer, he met his first serious girlfriend who worked as a bar attender in one of the clubs he did security. They hit it off from the start. She was a lot older than him and the sex was amazing. That is where his fascination and attraction with older women began. She was also better organised, lived in her own apartment while he was still living with his mother and sister.

She was working two jobs paying tuition to put her through university because she wanted to be a lawyer. For the first time in his life, he felt like he needed to be a man and step up to the plate and actually become something. She made him believe in himself and advised he tried looking for a job in sales since she noticed that he had a way with people.

She was not wrong because Reggie was a natural. When he was working at TW Home Improvements, he quickly became one of their best employees. With his big brown expressive eyes, those babies were his luck charms.

Like most typical clients who might have a preconceived mistrust for salespersons, he had a way of making them feel bad for mistrusting him. He would disarm his clients with his charming aura and features that would stop women in their tracks. Drawn to his Adonis look and careful flattery, clients would helplessly laugh at his jokes.

His untypical accent added to his mystique and as if they were under hypnosis, he guided them to the deals he wanted, while appearing to give them exactly what they required. As soon as they had signed the contract and paid the deposit, he would have forgotten their names and would be ready to enchant new customers. He had his method perfected down to a tee.

Bringing in so much revenue for the company and commission for himself, it only took him a short period to buy himself a car and move into his own apartment. The feeling he got from achieving these financial goals gave him a buzz, a drive and reason to live, it was a good addiction for him and the rewards needed to become greater.

Years later, he was offered an opportunity to be part of a new business which would require the same skills he possessed. In return, he would get a six-figure salary; travel benefits, an office of his own and an assistant. The prayers from his mother were truly being answered. Reggie took the job, moved his mother into a bigger spacious house and managed to support Esther with her career in music.

He and his girlfriend had started getting distant due to their strenuous working schedules, so they parted ways. When Reggie moved to his new place, she stopped coming over and he stopped calling. Their relationship was a weird one and Reggie often found himself struggling to define what it really was, so when it withered away, he didn't take no stock of it. After all, everything else was moving in the right direction.

After the death of their father, the family moved from Zimbabwe to start a new life in the United Kingdom. Their mother thought it would provide her kids with better opportunities even though she was also apprehensive about leaving everything she had grown to love behind, especially the church. She had an uncle who had moved straight to the UK from Mozambique back in the 70s and he had raised his kids there. He always used to send photographs and post cards.

Kainga used to be mesmerised by the beauty and serenity of rural England. She used to tell her uncle that the kids would have trouble adapting to the language and the general cold English weather. Her uncle would assure her that they would be alright. He also assured them that the cold English weather was not all year round. In fact, he deliberately always sent her pictures of his family in the summer to try and persuade them to come over.

When Reggie senior died mysteriously, Kainga felt like the family needed a change. There was nothing left for them in Zimbabwe, so she decided to emigrate to the UK on the grounds of reconciling with family. They got their visas approved in 1994 and in that same year, they moved to the UK. Reggie was 15 years old and Esther was 13. It didn't take long for the kids to integrate with the new community. They made friends in school, picked up sports and various activities. It really brought out the best in them and made them cope better with the loss of their father. It was a little harder for Kainga because she found it difficult to make new friends.

She did not particularly like the English food and found it difficult getting around places because it was hard for her to memorise bus routes. She admired the architecture of the buildings, but hated the fact that there was limited space to do the things she had been accustomed to.

She wanted to grow her own food, but she quickly found out that you sometimes needed to build a little greenhouse to nurse your plants. She also found that the way the people worshipped in the churches was different. There wasn't a lot of singing and if there was any, it was controlled and tamed.

To Kainga singing was a manifestation of the fullness of the spirit. She craved it; it was her medicine. From time to time, they would have their own little sermons in the house to cheer her up. Esther, who had always been good at playing musical instruments, played the piano. She had a Yamaha PS-10 electric keyboard to practice on and she would spend hours on it.

CHAPTER 4
In All Her Glory

T he size of the bedroom alone was huge with strategically placed furniture which even he could not tell where it was from. It looked damn expensive. The light coloured walls allowed natural light in and on them hung paintings by someone who obviously knew what they were doing. There was so much going on this room and it felt like it was almost impossible to take it all in a day. He poured himself a glass from the 40 years aged Louis the 13th Remy Martin cognac which was placed on a table a couple of feet from the bed.

Next to the bottle was expensive silver looking ladies' watch with shiny stones. He did not know what brand it was, but the logo was pretty interesting. He didn't put too much thought into it and he imagined it to be another useless piece of overpriced shit which told the same time as any.

You could hear the shower running in the background, but it was the soft jazz playing which created the erotic atmosphere. In all her glory she appeared from the steamed glass doors completely naked and stood in front of the big fireplace. There wasn't anything as sexy as seeing a powerful influential woman in this position ready to be fucked into submission. He was going to take his time, even if it meant holding out longer.

He knew it was going to be difficult because already his dick was hard and bulging through his pants. She slowly walked towards him and not once did he blink because he didn't want to miss a thing. She took the glass that he was holding and took a sip out of it before she placed it on the small table next to the Remy. He gently grabbed her by the waist, turned her so that his face was below her navel and started to lightly kiss her.

He gently made his way up to her plump breasts, making every single nerve in her body come alive with sexual tension. She had already started rubbing one of her nipples so he started licking the other causing it to pucker and tighten in his mouth. Her brown nipples made a sweet wet pop sound as he released them out of his mouth. He could feel her heart pounding as he kissed on the top of her soft chest. He stood upright and being much taller than her his ripped chest was right in front of her face.

She slowly unzipped his fly releasing his long thick penis, which she stroked gently as she went on her knees until she was able to put it in her mouth. She felt it grow stiffer in her mouth with its veins filling up. She started sucking on it simultaneously licking the tip and spitting on it making sure it was well polished with her spit. He held the back of her head and gently drove her into his dick until it felt like she was going to choke from it. Then she pulled it out of her mouth lifted the penis up and serviced the balls as well.

Melantha loved to suck dick and that alone would get her aroused. Her vagina was wet and she was ready to take him, but he wanted her to wait so he ordered her to lie on the bed on her back and started to use his tongue on her sensitive parts in slow unpredictable movements. She moaned a little yearning for more as he teased her, keeping her guessing how he was going to lick her next. He felt her clit harden which let him know that she was ready. Reggie gently guided his dick into her wetness and she opened her legs wider to accommodate all of him. Her vagina felt warm and tight he would not have imagined that she was almost 50. Truthfully, he didn't really know how old she was, but he knew she was way older than him. Even from under him, she rotated her hips rubbing his back and clutching on to his naked ass as he fucked her wildly. He felt her vagina envelope him causing him to thrust even harder sending pleasurable shock waves across her body. She exploded into a frenzied incoherent orgasm. They finished off with doggy style and he left her lying on the bed while he took a shower.

The mansion was in Tilton on the Hill about 20 miles away from the city. Everything about it was immaculate from the polished surfaces to the perfectly manicured lawns. You could see that it definitely took a big team of landscapers to keep it looking that good with all the flowers and hedges trimmed. It had to take a team of house cleaners to keep that mansion spotless like it was yet Reggie never saw anyone there.

 He understood that her husband had travelled overseas on business, but he expected to see a delivery driver dropping off a package, a workman finishing off some work, pest control or something. He knew she said she was being extra careful about their little rendezvous, but damn it just seemed bizarre. The more he thought about it that eerie feeling of being watched returned and made him step out the shower before he was done. He told Malantha once that he felt uncomfortable about them having sex at her house and he felt like someone was watching. She laughed it off and alluded to the fact that he was being paranoid.

She had an insatiable appetite for sex and so did he so this arrangement suited him just fine although he would have preferred to have the sexual escapades at his apartment. He never forced it because he figured a woman of her calibre probably got off on the thought of being fucked in that mansion. Thinking that her wealthy husband probably didn't fuck her as dirty as he did gave him a superman feeling.

Nevertheless, this wasn't enough to get his mind over the strange mansion. At some point he thought she would share with him ideas on how he could make himself as wealthy as she was, after all older women he had dealt with had given him pointers of some sort. He soon gave up on that notion because clearly Malantha's intentions were purely sexual. She was a professor of linguistics, fluent in many languages which were a turn on for Reggie. He wondered how many men she'd brought back from campus. He really didn't want to know besides worrying about that made him feel uncomfortable because apart from sex, fun and expensive Cognacs he didn't feel for her that much and that's why he was never truthful about where he worked when she asked.

Esther was trying her best to keep up with her brother, but she couldn't carry on running any longer, she needed a short break. They would meet at Victoria Park and do some stretches first before doing laps around the park. This was something they did occasionally and it was beneficial for Esther who struggled with weight issues since she was a little girl. She had been on many diets and tried different workout regimes, but nothing worked. Running was the only activity that gave her some sort of positive results so she stuck to it. These sessions gave them the opportunity to talk about what was going on in their lives.

"So how's the singing going sis, heard from mom that you really like doing backing vocals for the new band you joined."

"Yeah it's really going well we seem to be creating a buzz , we have a few gigs lined up locally and we'll be hitting the Glastonbury stage in June." "I'm so proud of you sis, I bet you're glad you stuck with it like I told you so I'm still waiting for a proper thank you" he said with a childish grin on his face. She laughed a little and said, "I got you bro. I know all you need is a couple of numbers from the pretty girls who follow us. All I have to say is, 'You're my brother'."

They both chuckled.

"We got an invite to play at that place you always talk about the umm, the Crypt."

"Oh yeah? Wow. How did you guys pull that off because I heard there's a waiting list?"

"We turned it down bro. You know the drummer Kong said he heard some stories about that place. He didn't want us to play there... weird stuff about someone being killed there years back."

"Really, you're sure it's that place, got to be some kind of joke you're sure it's that place sis, can't be I was there the other day with Chris and it was good."

"Kong and his family were literally born here bro so who knows he could be wrong or right. Maybe he meant some other bar. There's a few of them around that area and besides, he could have been high when he said that. To be honest, we all agreed not to do that gig, but only because we have been pretty much rehearsing every day. I guess we needed a break," she added.

They carried on talking for about 30 minutes about random stuff then they decided not finish the run "ate logo (see you later)" they said almost at the same time as they embraced before parting ways.

He mentioned to them that Wigston was one of the best places to live in Leicestershire. Besides the amazing rural feel they would be only 30 minutes away from East Midlands Airport. The M1 motorway was nearby so it provided easy links to both North and Southern destinations.

The newlyweds who were both professionals and first buyers wanted a comfortable property which was affordable and ideal to start a family. The detached cottage was on a cul-de-sac, the backyard was spacious complete with big apple trees ideal for kids and family get-togethers. He did his usual talk about how the amenities suited their requirements and he felt relaxed judging from their expressions that they were satisfied.

Reggie politely excused himself from the couple and went outside to make a call. He called his assistant wanting to schedule a meeting with the Deans at 3pm later on in the afternoon. The assistant informed him that they had already chosen a property and they were keen to get all the paperwork done to process the sale.

This was great news; he punched the air in celebration making sure his clients didn't see him. He reminded his assistant to tell them that he still needed to do a full viewing with them because it was procedure. They had picked a 1.5 million pound home which was going to be a good bonus for him.

He'd never caught feelings for any woman that's why his encounters were mostly casual, but since meeting Carmen the other night he felt a different kind of attraction, not just sexual. He wasn't used to that feeling it scared him that is why he hadn't followed up on her after the evening at the Crypt; it scared him in a good way though. Later that night he decided to text her instead of calling because he did not want to deal with the awkwardness of having to somehow explain why it took him so long to get in touch.

CHAPTER 5
Simukah Gorah

The spooky staircase led down to a dark passageway which smelt like crudely built medieval dry walls and timber. The first few times he'd ever walked down there he held on to the walls for guidance and the texture of the timber was reminiscent of William Shakespeare's house which he'd visited as a kid on a field trip with school in Stratford Upon Avon.

He walked past a wine cellar which hadn't been in use for a while judging by the dusty barrels and bottles. In front of him a doorway emerged on the left. There was a little light in that direction, candle light because the basement had no electrical wiring. From where he was the combination of the candle light flickering on the brick walls made the imagery look like grainy world war one footage. When he slowly walked there was a man standing in front with reddish cross on his neck and gaunt soulless eyes. There were alcoves were others stood in the shadows making it impossible to tell their faces.

They were holding walking staffs made from human bones with both their hands holding the top part of the sticks, which were shaped into a cross that was similar to the man who was at the front.

It was customary to lick the four fingers of your left hand and run them down another kumoz neck showing allegiance to the deity. This was part of their tradition, which they had practiced since the beginning of the Neolithic period. Cilo Secret Society practiced their tradition of acquiring fortune and tremendous wealth by practicing cilocy. This involved making hurumbo sacrifices to the Gorah who was their guardian and protector.

They went around each other murmuring, "blessed are the destroyers of fear and chance, cursed are those who think God will intervene for they shall be shorn the power of Gorah" in emotionless voices. They wore black cloaks with loose hoodies, which covered the nose and mouth only leaving their emotionless eyes and neck exposed.

"Simukah Gorah, Simukah Gorah, Simukah Gorah" the man in the front kept saying commanding the poltergeist to make its presence felt and the more he kept repeating those words the air got tighter and colder as the demonic presence filled the space.

His eyes began to get blood shot and his voice began to change into a sinister growl with an icy undertone. Blood came out from the cloth covering his nose and mouth going down to his neck.

His eyes too had transformed into complete red with blood coming out from them. All the kumoz knelt before him saying the words Simukah Gorah under their breath until his face was totally covered in blood.

"It's time," he said.

CHAPTER 6
Mr Dean

Her scent was sweet, fruity, reminding him of the aroma of freshly sliced peaches his mom used to pick. She wore an outfit which looked sexy, but not easy. They sat outside at Ricardo's, a pizza spot in the city on Bath lane overlooking the River Soar.

The sound of the calm water was like a quiet blow to the skin. Reggie was not sure if she would have liked going to a pizza spot, when he sent the text message he only mentioned the location, but from the look on her face it seemed she was comfortable.

He'd made it a point to make it a day date rather than a night date because most of his night dates ended up leading to the bedroom. Alcohol always had a way of fuelling lechery so he was having some pop instead. He genuinely wanted to know more about Carmen without his dick dictating his actions.

She thought his brown skin glowed under the day light bringing out the warm orange and red undertones. She found it hard to determine the one feature which made Reggie handsome. He had the right balance of intensity and gentleness. Carmen liked his eyes from the first time she met him at the crypt. She could tell he worked out even when she'd only ever seen him in, button downs. After having pizza, they spoke about their childhood and work.

Reggie could sense that she wasn't giving too much away, he did most of the talking. Like little kids they giggled when they found out that they'd both had the Sega Genesis mega drive as kids. Her favourite game was Sonic and Knuckles and Reggie's was Warlock. She hated old furniture though and found it hilarious that he could almost name the century and make of most antique furniture.

 He showed off a little by saying the chairs they were sat on were Georgian made in the 18th century and worth quite a bit of money. She rolled her eyes at him then he learned over and whispered that they were actually replicas and again they chuckled. He also asked how her friend Freya was and she said she was fine even though they hadn't hung out or spoken much after the other night.

He said the same about Chris except they spoke a lot more often and Chris would always try to get him to go out drinking. This was the type of man she saw herself with. Not the stuck up controlling spoiled rich brats her parents preferred her to date. To her they had no clue of what being a real man was about. Their idea of a woman's happiness was only connected to pounds, dollars and Euros.

From that day onwards they spoke and texted each other daily. Carmen made him feel like he didn't want to speak or spend any time with any other woman besides her. This was a new feeling to him and it gave him purpose. He invited her over to his apartment, prepared some steak and salad and they had a bottle of red wine.

He had an extensive collection of music from all the Motown classics, jazz and some old records like Orchestra Marrabenta Starr de Mocambique which reminded him of his dad. He was more into Kizomba music which was a modern genre sung in Portuguese it had a romantic, sensuous and slow rhythmic feel.

He pulled out Nelson Freitas's Elevate CD and went to Track 9 called 'Life is Good'. She sat watching him as he moved backwards and forwards with a slight tilt in his waist. His sexy body swayed from side to side as he executed some smooth kizomba dance moves. It was so enticing and made him look like a male stripper; after all he had the body for it. Reggie bit both his lips as his movements intensified in harmony with the song.

She sat there grinning holding her glass of red wine with her legs crossed trying not to give away what she felt. He extended his hand for her to join in and his expressions were clear that he wasn't going to take no for an answer. He took her left and right hand and asked her to follow his lead. He placed his hand on Carmen's back and instructed her to place her left hand on his shoulder then he looked straight into her eyes.

He stepped forward with his left foot while guiding her with his body to go back on her right foot followed by a slight pause then the same again on the opposite side till she got the basic momentum of it. They did it a couple of times before the music changed to track 10 called drinks on me. By this time she was well into the swing of it. Anticipating his movements their grips got tighter and their hips touched with intense sexual energy she closed her eyes engulfed in euphoria.

The scent of their bodies mixed in with the aroma of the red wine on their breaths enhanced their yearning for each other. Their lips met and he had his fingers in her hair. As the kissing intensified their tongues wrestled flooding their bodies with immense charges.

With their lips still united, they frantically undressed down to the skin and Reggie carried her into the bedroom. Carmen spent the night at Reggie's apartment and he made breakfast in the morning. It was definitely the best time they'd both had in a while and Reggie knew that this woman had to be special.

He spotted a blue 2012 Rolls Royce Phantom coupe parked on the drive, in front of the Seven Oaks mansion on 563 Bradgate Road in Newtown Linford. As he pulled up behind it he checked the time to see if he was late and he wasn't in fact he was about 15 minutes early. This was a habit he had in case anything needed straightening before clients arrived. There wasn't anyone in front of the house so they must have been in the back because he had the house keys.

"You must be Mr Dean, I'm Reggie from Pegasus," he said with a warm friendly smile. He walked towards Mr Dean who had already turned in his direction when he heard his footsteps then they shook hands. He had a real firm handshake for a 60 something year old man. His clothes were classic and understated, very sophisticated indeed yet there was something about this man which was not right even when he smiled it looked forced. As he was juggling these thoughts he had a familiar voice say, "We like the house".

When he shifted his eyes to look at who it was his whole body went stiff when he saw Malantha emerge from a wall next to the guesthouse.

His mouth went dry instantly like a marathon runner's except he wasn't thirsty he was confused. It almost made him drop the house keys. It wasn't until he felt Mr Dean's cold hand on his shoulder when he snapped back into reality realising that these two must have been husband and wife. "What the fuck!" he thought to himself at the same time as Mr Dean said, "Yes, we really like the house darling, are you going to show us inside Reggie."

"Yes, yes of course," he said involuntarily clearing his throat, trying his best to disguise the fact that he was still shook. He avoided eye contact with Malantha because he did not want to give away the fact that they knew each other. He suggested they made their way round to the front of the house so they could see the inside. To counter the anxiety, he found himself going into more detail about the Baroque style mansion with marble floors, grand staircases and barrel-vaulted coffered ceilings.

What was even more surprising to him was that during the whole tour of the house, Malantha did not show any signs of discomfort or awkwardness at all. In fact, her whole demeanour was rather suggestive. She flaunted her sexy body around and perked her breasts as though she was auditioning for a porno film.

She sure had a repertoire of seductive tricks and he wondered if she had any limits. Without a doubt, this was going to be the biggest deal he facilitated, so he was excited about it even though the viewing was like torture.

At that point, all he wanted to do was close the deal as quickly as possible so he wouldn't have to see Malantha and her creepy husband again. He imagined how Carmen would feel if she ever found out about Malantha. He would do anything in his power to make sure she never found out. "So all that's left to do is getting the paperwork done, I will email you a form explaining all the fees which need to be settled, and when you come back to the office we can close, how does that sound?" directing all the questions to Mr Dean.

"I look forward to it," Mr Dean responded extending his hand for a handshake.

Reggie noticed he had a male version of the watch he had seen at their house next to the Cognac bottle the other day. The whole situation was total mind fuck. He shook both their hands as best composed as he could and they all returned to their vehicles. Reggie went and pulled out the home for sale sign on the grass and tossed it in the back of the car. Mr Dean waved at him and it sent chills down his spine because his whole energy was empty he was glad when they finally drove off.

CHAPTER 7
Vasco Da Gama

The stair master is definitely one of those machines you think twice about going on because it makes you sweat buckets. Reggie recommended it to everyone especially when people asked how he stayed so ripped all year round. To take his mind off the agony, he favoured the machines closer to the big plasma screens which were mounted on the wall in front. It was also the best section of the gym to watch women because they always flooded the machines in their tight gym wear. On the screens, they showed the BBC news. The sound was muted, but the subtitles were on, so he casually read them even though he paid no attention to what was being said.

To him, the news always showed depressing stuff. On that day, they showed images of the destruction caused by Typhoon Haiyan in the Philippines where homes were completely destroyed. The images of women and children being interviewed saddened him, so he looked away briefly waiting for something else to come on.

This time there was a lady on the screen with subtitles indicating that police had been called to Victoria Park where the body of a woman had been found. This immediately caught his attention because he seldom went jogging there with Esther. He knew it wouldn't have been Esther because they had texted when he woke up. He carried on reading the sub titles and they went into detail about how the runners came across the body and how police were collecting evidence and treating it as a homicide.

They appealed for anyone who had any information to contact them then they spoke about all the other stuff police talk about in similar incidences. He thought how ironic it was that none of the women in the gym were watching this or paying attention to the fact that there was a potential serial killer on the loose. They were all consumed with their exercise and whatever music they were listening to through their headphones. In the changing room Reggie sent a text messages to people he cared about starting with Carmen and he smiled to himself when he got an instant response from her.

There'd always been mystery surrounding the death of their father and their mother never explained what happened they rarely talked about it because it used to upset her. They loved their father, but he was a secretive and mysterious man even to his kids. This is something they grew to accept about him.

They knew he had escaped some type of family situation in Portugal. His family had been part of a group of special people who had great influence and their blood line traced back to the great Portuguese explorer Vasco Da Gama who arrived in Mozambique in the 15th Century. It was documented that their voyage had been one of the longest and toughest expeditions, especially when they sailed across the Mediterranean and treacherous Arabian Peninsula.

Myth had it that King Manuel I handed the captains of the Portuguese armada sealed wooden boxes with crosses on them. The captains were instructed to only open the boxes when faced with potentially life threatening situations. They would have also had to sacrifice two crewmen as part of the pact. To this day no one really knows if this was true or not because some say it never happened while others say it did. King Manuel I who was ruler of Portugal at that time was known to employ cunning tactics on his subordinates as a way of instilling loyalty, fear and bravery.

Around the discovery of the Cape of Good Hope Vasco Da Gama and his men were plagued with scurvy and they had limited supplies left. He lost a lot of his men to the plague which made the sufferers bodies disintegrate. Blisters formed all over the skin and broke out into full-blown ulcers. They threw the bodies of the dead overboard to limit the spread of the disease and to keep the smell away.

When fierce battles broke out between them and the Arab ships fatalities increased. The ships used big iron grappling-hooks fixed to chains to draw each other closer for hand to hand combat. Crewmen used ballista and shot crossbows while others deployed the use of bludgeons. The gruesomeness of the clashes under the violence and roughness of the sea meant that even though Da Gama and his men won there were only a few left to complete the voyage so he ended up opening the box and sacrificing two men to the cause. After the gory incident everything else about the voyage was a success. Others believed that the sacrificing became customary even after the wars. In recent times when the sacrificing of humans became a crime the practice was more underground and manifested the emergence of a secret society which Reggie senior's grandparents and parents were a part of.

Ever since the house viewing with the Deans, Reggie had met them one last time to seal the deal on their house. It had been three weeks since then. He avoided any contact with Malantha, but she was not taking the hint. She kept on leaving him voice messages and texts. She was like a pimple on the nose, which wouldn't go away.

He hadn't blocked her number completely, fearing she would show up at his job or apartment. She was that kind of crazy. Putting his phone away he grabbed a copy of the Leicester Mercury and folded it before going into Starbucks and ordering his usual triple venti latte. When he sat down and unfolded the newspaper to read he was shocked to see a familiar face on the front page.

The headlines read that police had released the identity of the person whose body had been found at the park weeks earlier. Her name was Freya Kunis. Without reading the rest of the story he immediately called Chris to tell him what he had saw.

"Have you seen the headlines in the paper today Chris?" he said, knowing that as a local businessman he was an avid reader of *The Mercury*.

"Hi Reggie what's up? No, I haven't seen it. Why?"

"You need to look at it man. They said the body of the woman found at Victoria Park is Freya."

There was a short silence followed by a response from Chris.

"That's really sad. I hadn't heard from her in a long while. I wonder what happened."

Still in disbelief, Reggie explained how he had seen the story on the news and never imagined it would have been anyone he knew.

Chris mentioned that he had seen it too and said Freya was not a jogger, so they both wondered what she was doing at the park.

They agreed to meet later to discuss it further, but Reggie was perplexed by the blasé reaction Chris had about the whole thing. For someone who knew Freya more than him, he just sounded unmoved.

He even remembered Carmen saying Freya and Chris once had a fling though Reggie thought she wasn't his usual type. When Reggie rang Carmen, the news had already got to her and she was inconsolable. Further reading confirmed their suspicions about the murder having been committed elsewhere. Her body had been dumped at the park and she had a typical office dress on, indicating that she wasn't jogging. Her body was also described as having weird cuts and lacerations.

Reggie called his boss and told him that he was not going to come into work for the day. His head was all over the place. He felt like something was not adding up and it was messing with his head. He decided to go to The Crypt for a drink, as he thought it would give him some sort of closure. He also thought that since he had first met Freya there, it would be a way of paying his respects. The place was empty since it was midweek.

There was no music playing or anything going on. It gave off a sinister energy which he had never felt before and he didn't know if it was to do with the current state of affairs.

Reggie felt like it may have been because of what Esther had told him weeks back about the place being tied to a murder. Like a claustrophobic he felt his whole being urging him to leave so he left his drink and made his way into the car park.

While gathering his thoughts and trying to figure out what had transpired he saw Chris coming out of the back door on the side leading to the car park. This was strange because when they spoke earlier Chris had told him that he was in Birmingham. For a minute he thought he was seeing things till he watched Chris getting into his grey Panamera with private plates.

It was definitely him and he seemed like he was in a panic. He drove right past Reggie without even noticing his vehicle. Reggie squinted his eyes to focus on the image of a tall skinny man in dark clothing walking out the same door "the hell" he said to himself realising that it was Mr Dean walking to the familiar Rolls Royce which was parked in his blind spot.

Those gunmetal eyes were recognisable from a distance. His whole heinous overtone could be felt from a distance. Like a cop on stakeout, Reggie sank in his seat to avoid detection as the Rolls Royce swept past him.

CHAPTER 8
Will You Mary Me

"Blessed are the destroyers of fear and chance, cursed are those who think god will intervene for they shall be shorn the power of Gorah", the kumoz said . The man in front was the Gorah's incarnate who when summoned by the Kumoz his face would start dripping blood.

He would groan and gibber in a gruffy voice giving instructions on what needed doing as far as Cilocy was concerned. There was a hierarchy system with the oldest serving members being on top down to the least serving and it was up to this hierarchy system to decide who joined.

Membership was only open to aristocrats. Different offerings were made to pledge allegiance to the Gorah and once you became a member it was for life and your family would be bound in it forever. They were part of a global secret society with members in all segments of government in every country.

"You know horombo is due on the seventh Friday from today. I have received my first and now I await my second. The correct steps have already been made.

"All of you have played an important role in keeping our cause at the forefront of your lives. In return, I give you grails of never-ending wealth and success for your families. The way non-believers crave water to sustain life, is the same way we crave blood. Without it what has been keeping us alive, prosperous and in control will cease to exist.

"I await the blood. I await the blood. I await the blood. I know you will deliver as always."

He raised both his hands and the kumoz started chanting, "Simukah Gorah, Simukah Gorah, Simukah Gorah."

He slowly retreated to one of the many alcoves in the basement, and the Kumoz started to disperse.

During the succession, one of the kumoz had been nervous because his plans where not going smoothly, but he was careful not to let it show in the presence of the Gorah. The task of delivering the sacrifice had been given to him, but he was finding it difficult to deliver on his promise. Usually by now, they would have had their sacrifice under their watchful eye at any one of their holding facilities. He decided to think of a way to make his plans come to fruition faster and easier. Once the meeting was over he made a phone call.

To get their minds off what had been happening, Reggie and Carmen decided to make weekend reservations at Armathwaite Hall off the beaten track in Cumbria. They figured the combination of its low-key location, spa and outdoor activities was exactly what it would take to clear their minds and get them closer together without the distractions of the city.

They drove up there on a Friday afternoon via the A1, which is a long 3-hour journey. By the time they got there, it was dark so they checked in and had a bottle of wine before falling asleep in each other's arms.

The water cascaded down Carmen's hair and all over, her curves and the fresh breeze coming in from the large windows brushed her nipples making them hard and pointy. She could sense his eyes looking at her body inch by inch even with her eyes closed. He moved closer to her and she could feel his breathe on her neck below her ear and it sent sexual vibrations right through her spine. She felt his long thick dick poking her as they started to kiss through the gashes of the shower water.

She was lost in reverie until he bent her over and started to gently lick her pussy lips with his hands on her firm cheeks. She spread her legs apart and bent over even more as he started to tease her clit with his warm tongue. Even with the water running he could taste her juices. He felt the tremble in her legs so he gently helped her stand and picked her up putting her against the shower wall. Carmen reached for his dick and guided it into her wet pussy. She wrapped her legs around his waist.

They started to hungrily kiss while he made semi-circle motions inside her with his cock. He washed his face with her breasts and gently thrust into her. She kept asking for more so he increased the intensity. The water splashed off from their clapping bodies creating an unsynchronized erotic noise. His strong hands moved interchangeably from her thighs and ass while she clanged on to him like her life depended on it. Moments later their bodies fell into a wild frenzy and they both moaned and exploded into climax.

"Honestly who wears those for horse riding" Carmen said letting out a loud laugh pointing at the pair of dragon Adidas Reggie had on. "Well they're comfortable and when I read the manual they said wear comfortable shoes, so I did" he said laughing right along with Carmen who wore sexy tight fitting blue jeans and brown sovereign high rider boots. They made their way down to the front of the hotel were a coach was waiting to take them to the nearby stables.

On their way to Cumbria past Stoke on Trent they noticed a black Range Rover had been on their tail for quite a distance, but they paid little attention to it. They saw a similar vehicle when they took a break on the M61 services, but they were unsure if it was the same one. Carmen always spoke about how she grew up riding horses on her parent's farm.

She told him that she didn't like going there anymore because of the difference in opinions they had about her future. Reggie imagined himself meeting her parents one day and maybe being the peacemaker between them, but he never pushed her to talk about them. He just figured time would fix things.

After the horse ride they hired a boat and slowly rowed on the calm Bassenthwaite Lake. The sunset gave the water an orange glow which reflected off the crystal water creating an enchanting aura.

The water was very quiet now and the boat felt almost still when Reggie opened a bottle of vintage wine and said, "Since the day I met you, I have changed in ways I never thought possible. I was used to just floating along with whatever life threw at me and even though it felt empty I stopped trying to figure out why it felt empty."

"That is until I met you, Carmen you have completed me and have made me realise that all I needed to be complete was you."

"I love you, I love you so much. What I'm trying to say is I want to spend the rest of my life with you. Carmen Rosario will you marry me?" He said, holding a classic four-claw solitaire 18-karat white gold ring he had concealed in his jacket.

"Yes, yes Reggie," she said with tears of joy flowing down her cheeks.

They were now driving back and the roads were clear since it was a Sunday. Carmen sat on the passenger side while Reggie drove. There wasn't any music playing and it was just fine because their thoughts were loud enough. They were so comfortable with each other to the point where even silent moments felt warm and pleasant.

All that could be heard was the muted hum of the car tearing across the wide lane motorway which was as straight as dried spaghetti. She was having full conversations with herself imagining how her wedding would be, how her dress would look.

She was so happy and safe with the man she loved and felt glad to have waited for him instead of settling for the type of men her parents wanted for her. She was in full day dreaming mode looking through the car windows. The tall trees undulated gently in the breeze and she would catch herself smiling through her reflection.

In Reggie's utopia he saw a house with kids and a dog. He pictured his mother in the kitchen with his wife baking some biscuits. He would look at Carmen then look at the sparkling rock on her finger and they would both giggle like teenage couples on prom night.

The day progressed smoothly and they drove past Doncaster along the A1 southbound and when they got to the island to switch on to the M18. The road was closed due to some road construction. "Why have we slowed down?" Carmen asked waking up from a long nap which had been halted by the change in momentum. "Damn traffic diversion" he said while cursing under his breath to disguise his obvious frustration.

"It's alright sweetie go back to sleep," he said gently rubbing her shoulder and adjusting the sweater she had been covering herself with. They were some traffic diversion signs directing traffic to an alternative route. Reggie took a right into a narrow road where the arrows pointed and continued to drive.

The road was quiet in fact for the last 10 miles he'd only driven past two cars headed in the opposite direction, but none followed behind him. He was starting to feel a little tired, but there was nowhere to stop. Usually this would have been the perfect time to play music, but he did not want to wake Carmen up.

Therefore, he decided to entertain himself by silently counting how many cars he would come across before connecting back on to the M18. He adjusted his rear view mirror and spotted a car at a distance driving towards them and casually counted "one" then refocused his attention ahead. This road was not as wide as the motorway. Moments later, Reggie looked in his rear view mirror again and thought he recognised the car which was fast approaching. He squinted his eyes a little to sharpen his focus while re-adjusting the mirror which was already correctly aligned. He recognized the same black Range Rover which they had seen three days ago.

He nudged Carmen to wake up so she could confirm if it was indeed the same car. She looked behind and immediately confirmed that it was. Reggie slowed down hoping the car would drive right passed them since the road was clear.

There hadn't been any oncoming traffic for miles. To his surprise the car seemed to slow down as well. It was tailgating them and it was so close that they couldn't make out the registration plates and when Reggie put his foot on the gas to accelerate, the car behind did the same. Filled with anxiety, mixed with fear of being at the mercy of the car behind them, they were both quiet yet extremely uncomfortable fidgeting in their seats while keeping an eye on the Range Rover. Reggie started to feel for his cell phone so he could try and call someone and that's when the car pulled past them and got in front.

They both noticed that the driver was not alone, he had a passenger, but the car had blacked out windows so they could not tell if there were passengers in the back seats. The registration plates had been covered in dirt possibly accumulated during the long drive. It was difficult to make out the numbers and letters, especially as the car sped off in full speed as if it was now challenging them to a race.

"What the hell was that?" Reggie screamed in an unusual tremulous tone after noticing that the car had disappeared into the horizon "fuck! Are you ok baby? ", he asked looking at Carmen who was scrambling in her bag looking for her phone so she could call her parents. She was visibly shaken and you could see her heart hammer against her chest. She just nodded and dialled her dad's number, but the signal was low so the call did not go through.

Carmen tossed the phone back in the bag and grabbed his arm trying her best to withhold tears.

The thoughts of taking a break or possibly stopping for some food were overpowered by those of getting to Leicester as soon as possible and it was starting to get dark.

As their nerves were starting to calm down, the quietness was interrupted by a loud tremendous hit. This made their bodies erratically jolt forward and loose items in the car got tossed to the front. If it wasn't for the seatbelts they would have been thrown out through the wind shield. Carmen was screaming something, but Reggie could not hear it for he was now holding the steering wheel desperately with both hands trying to avoid veering off the road.

The vehicle behind rammed into them again causing them to almost lose control, but Reggie's senses and awareness were now heightened so he regained control and stepped on the gas. You could hear wheels screeching and pieces of metal and glass falling off the vehicles.

Carmen held on to the door handle tighter than a first time skydiving student with tears rolling down her face. They could clearly see that it was the black Range Rover again and it was catching up to them making another attempt to bulldoze them off the road. The Range Rover Vogue was a much larger vehicle compared to their BMW 520i so if it went to the side of them they would be eventually overpowered and forced into the trees Reggie thought.

He glanced at his dials and he was doing over 100mph at this point their only chance was to out speed the Range hoping they would soon reach a built up area or run into a police car.

They smelt the rubber from the tyres working overtime and Carmen started to yell, "Oh my God Reggie, go faster," looking at the Range, which was starting to gain on them.

"Fuck, this is all I got," briefly looking on his right noticing the black car attempt to clip him on the rear fender.

Part of its front was now missing making it difficult for the driver to catch the left back end of the BMW, which had also caved in. Whoever was in the other car was definitely trying to take them out, but Reggie was determined to go down with a fight.

The cat and mouse chase carried on for a mile and just as the Range Rover had gotten on their side in the perfect position to side swipe them a dazzling glare filled the windshields of both cars followed by loud horns for about 50 seconds. Reggie and Carmen recognised the headlights of a big euro truck just before it ploughed into the Range Rover sending it flying on the other side of the road. Almost in sequence, the back tyre on their car blew up causing the car to fish tail.

Carmen screamed on top of her lungs as Reggie tried to control the car, but the vehicle spun out of control in a huge cloud of smoke as car parts littered the road.

Moments later, there was extreme silence like a piercing sound in your ear silence. Everything appeared disorientated, from the Range Rover, which had dropped in a ravine to the overturned BMW in the middle of the road with two people in it who were not moving. Like the aftermath of a heated gunfire exchange on a battlefield, the scene was quiet and surreal.

CHAPTER 9
Meet The In-Laws

Multiple scenes of conversations with a man, people gathered together and snippets of the accident began to flash in his head. The thoughts dissolved into nothing and for at least one minute in his mind he saw a long black tunnel followed by a single deafening beeping sound. When he became conscious opening his eyes some fluorescent lights shined down on him. So bright were the lights that his pupil constricted fast intensifying the pain he felt in his head. There was a man dressed in white and his face was silhouetted by the lights. He thought he was dead, in the afterlife looking at an angel.

"Sir, Sir, Do you know what happened to you?" he wanted to nod, but his head felt too heavy for his neck muscles to control. The man told him not to try and make any rapid movements except to blink if he understood what he was saying, blinking once to say yes and twice to say no. "Do you know you were involved in a serious car accident? "he responded by blinking once, "you are very lucky to be alive without any life threatening injuries even though you are in pain right now." "What I'm about to tell you is not good, but we have to tell you. Unfortunately the other person did not make it sir, I'm very sorry." He began to blink many times and tears started to form crystallising his vision while he went back to sleep from the powerful painkillers which had been administered earlier.

"Didn't I tell you that it was too damn risky? There are other ways it could have been done, now look at the mess we're in" Malantha said slamming the phone down and finishing her cognac with one single gulp. "You have to clean it up as soon as possible before things get out of hand, now let's go!"

After a period of no conversation at all between them, Mr Dean broke the silence, "You know time is running out and this has to be done or we risk losing everything."

Malantha did not respond she just sat there emotionless. Not even the annoying voice of the car's gps made her react. They were heading off to Royal Hallamshire Hospital in Sheffield were the call had come from. The whole 70-mile journey was filled with silence until they got to the Hospital reception to make enquiries.

Reggie had sustained two broken ribs and minor bruising so the nurses were wheeling him to the recovery ward when he caught sight of a couple he least expected to see ever again, especially at a hospital out of town.

It was Malantha and Mr Dean. "The hell," he whispered to himself turning his head away from their direction so they wouldn't clock him.

He got assisted on to the bed by two nurses who talked to him about his medicines, time tables for food, how to operate his bed and remote for the TV. He smiled with gratitude and maintained eye contact with the nurses to show that he was with them when in reality he was mentally checked-out pondering about the Deans.

"Father, thank you for always being present in our lives. Thank you for protecting Reggie and keeping him away from the devil's claws. What an amazing God we serve, we know there is healing in your gentle touch. Through the suffering of Christ, we ask for your restoration and trust in your goodness. Our Saviour, our Healer, who brings forgiveness and hope.

"May life and wellness grow in fullness for Reggie and Carmen, healer and redeemer Jesus Christ Amen."

Kainga and Esther were standing on either side of Reggie's bed. He was clearly looking and feeling a lot better. His mother's prayers always made him feel protected and he was glad that she kept her voice low because he didn't want to get embarrassed in front of the other patients.

He knew his mom was one not to hold back especially when caught by the Holy Ghost, but he was happy to see them both. They were still holding hands when Reggie said in a low tone so the other patients wouldn't hear, "The food here is horrible".

Esther and Kainga burst out laughing making the nurse in charge look at them with talking eyes.

"You should have brought me some cozido a portuguesa," he said.

"Remember that time you had a full plate of it and fell asleep for three hours soon after?" said Esther playfully.

"Here you go again with that same old story sis I was only ten," Reggie responded while fixing his pillows with his mom helping him so he could sit up straight.

They were pleased to see him in good spirits so they intentionally avoided talking about details of the accident instead they decided to strictly dwell on the positive.

"I'm so happy for you and Carmen Reggie, you did the right thing and about time you settle down", we saw Carmen before we came here and thank God both of you will be discharged soon."

Reggie had been checking on her fiancé regularly since they had been admitted. Apart from a few fractured bones she had suffered a serious concussion so she did not remember a lot of what happened. He didn't care, he was happy that she remembered him and she was alive. That is all that mattered to him. Visiting hours were almost over and around this time the nurse in charge would start asking people to exit the ward. They hugged Reggie and told him that they would drive down and pick him up in two days which was their discharge date then they headed for the exit. Esther went running back to his bed. Kainga rolled her eyes and carried on walking towards the double swing doors. She knew her children were very close, even if visits would have been 8hours long those two wouldn't run out of things to talk about.

The nurse in charge was busy dealing with relatives of a patient on the adjacent bed so she didn't see Esther run back to the bad. Reggie was quietly giggling to himself because all this was entertainment for him.

"By the way we met Carmen's parents today, the Deans and they are lovely, love you," she said with genuine excitement before carefully sneaking to the door without arousing the nurse's attention. Everything from the sounds, the smells and even the movements in the ward just froze. It felt like he was stuck in a floating time dimension.

His face crumpled with confusion. He slid his body back into bed and this made is hospital clothes wrinkle up to his face. He tightly bit into the top part of them making him look more like a mental health patient. His mind state grew into disarray and the state of confusion made way for insomnia. He even started talking to himself trying to comprehend the fact that his in-laws were the Deans. It now made sense to him why he had seen them at reception the other day. They had come to visit their daughter.

He felt disgusted with himself knowing he had been involved with Malantha who was now his mother in law. It made him physically sick. He also had moments when he felt betrayed. He thought Carmen should have told him who her parents were. She always avoided talking about them at all costs. He wondered why she used Rosario as her surname instead of Dean. That would have been an easier way to connect the dots.

This was the lowest point he'd ever reached in his life. He felt like digging a hole and burying himself under because there was no coming back from this. Even his mom would not have been able to pray this one away and if she knew he had slept with his mother in law she would never look at him the same. Never mind his family he imagined Carmen never wanting to see him again and it crushed him. He needed to speak to someone who would give him independent advice. He grabbed his phone, walked outside and dialled Chris's number, but his phone kept going straight to voicemail. Chris knew more about Carmen's background more than he did. He remembered that he'd also seen him walking out of the Crypt from a possible conversation with Mr Dean. The confusion made him feel like a fly trapped trying hard to fly through a window to get outside.

Reggie found himself craving anything alcoholic, but he was in hospital so he had to cope with his thoughts. He was standing in the smoking area when another patient came out to smoke he asked for a cigarette and lighter. He put the cigarette on his lips and struggled to light it up. The other patient lit it up for him and they both started smoking in complete silence. He held his head in his hands wondering what he would say or do when he saw Carmen again.

A text message tone followed by a strong vibration alert went off. Reggie unlocked his phone and read the text message from his fiancé. "Hi Reggie, I can't wait to get out of here and get our life back, are you ready to go?" He responded saying "Hi sweetie, me too I'm ready." "Reggie are you sure you're ok, you've been distant for the past couple of days." He texted back saying he was ok and he was trying to figure out what had really happened. She texted back consoling him and urging him to try and stop thinking about it too much.

They were both scheduled for discharge in the afternoon and Carmen had suggested they go back to Leicester in her parent's car. He had liked the idea and thought it would have been the perfect opportunity to meet them. This was before he knew who they were. So he kindly declined the offer giving the excuse that they probably needed to spend quality time together since she had been spending most of her time with him. He told her that they would catch up in Leicester and this would also allow him to spend time with his family. In his mind he needed to keep his distance from Carmen while he figured out how to best handle the whole situation.

Esther was driving, Kainga was in the front passenger seat and Reggie was in the backseat. They could tell that he was not himself, but to them it was obvious why he wasn't. After all it normally takes months even years for people who have been in serious accidents to recover. They also knew that Reggie was the type who hated sympathy and pity so they tried to keep him occupied with small talk. "I told the guys in the band that you'd been to Wales and they said it was a beautiful place to visit, next time you should invite me along" Esther said looking at him through the rear view mirror.

Reggie smiled looking back at her through the mirror trying to think of what to say. Before he opened his mouth she said, "Let me guess, out of the three of you I bet it was Carmen who made the suggestion to go there. She knows all the classy sophisticated places."

Without allowing her to finish her sentence, Reggie asked, "What do you mean 'out of the three of us'? It was only me and Carmen."

From the look on his face, they could tell he was dead serious. Judging from the look of Esther's and Kainga's faces, he could tell they too were also serious.

"Esther what do you mean us three?" Her face twisted into a scowl, but since they weren't arguing, he figured she was confused.

"Well when we arrived at the hospital we ran into your good friend Chris and he seemed to have been discharged as well so we assumed you guys were together."

"Wait what, you saw Chris where?"

There was a mystified look in his eyes. He was puzzled, but he remembered something. It was actually Chris who had recommended the Armathwaite Hall saying that some of his clients had been there and they liked it. When Reggie asked if they spoke to Chris, they said they only managed to greet him because he looked shaken which they assumed was from the ordeal. An elderly man and a younger man came to pick him up.

Kainga and Esther assumed it was his dad and brother.

"You've had your fair share of weirdo friends, but Chris might be the worst," Esther said.

When Reggie did not say anything more, they concluded that they may have been together. The doctor had mentioned that Reggie could have short-term memory loss and the shock could make him omit certain moments.

"Try and sleep a little," Kainga said. Reggie just nodded and adjusted his sitting position to a slight lean so he could sleep and that's when he realised there was more to Chris than he knew.

Chapter 10
Vacheron Constantin

They were clearing the house getting it ready for the next meeting because after the discovery of the dead body in the park weeks earlier, certain information had leaked so they had to find a new place to gather. They had cleared the basement to make space for the people coming. Mr Dean had his black gown laid on the bed ready for him to wear. If someone would have seen it they would have thought it was a graduation gown and someone was getting ready to graduate except this gown had a red cross around the neck area. He wore his Vacheron Constantin automatic Swiss watch which they had agreed that every member should wear with no exceptions.

The watch had a cross emblem and came in many designs from leather strapped ones either in gold, silver or bimetal. If an unsuspecting person was to walk in room full of Cilocy members they wouldn't pick up the connection, but the members recognised each other that way in any part of the world. Their members were in all areas of high society from the police, courts and business executives.

Rodrigo Dentas as he was known as a young man grew up in a wealthy family who were part of a long line of Cilocy members. His father had picked him as the chosen one. His father had the ability to be the Gorah's reincarnate delivering the deity's messages to the Kumoz. The same gift was passed down to Rodrigo Dentas who as a child did not know what the dreams he thought were nightmares meant. From the description of his first dream to his father, the family knew he was the one.

In the beginning, he didn't know how to control the newfound skill so he was labelled as a social outcast due to his demeanour. Before his father died he taught him everything about reincarnating the Gorah. The way he took over the reins was like fish to water. He rose up in society and owned a few establishments including the infamous Crypt bar.

They were rumours of bizarre occurrences at the Crypt and whenever people asked questions the police chief would always dismiss them as ludicrous baseless gossip. This did not stop people from going there which provided the perfect cover for what was really going on in the basement. Amongst other nefarious activities, human sacrifices were common practice.

Some Kumoz disguised as patrons would always be in the crowd low key looking for easy targets based on the tips they would have received from members in the local police. They would target people who sold drugs or escorted so that when they came up missing they would orchestrate blaming their deaths on lifestyle choices.

Horombo was fast approaching and the second sacrifice hadn't been secured. The Kumoz had done their usual greeting and chants they were now commanding the poltergeist to make its presence felt.

"Simukah Gorah, Simukah Gorah, Simukah Gorah" Chris chanted along with the other Kumoz, this was the only time he was glad to have the walking staff because it helped him shift his weight while walking. After the accident he started having back pain so on that day having the stick was a blessing. He owed a lot of his success to Cilocy and Mr Dean had been a close friend to his late father so their bond was strong. This is why when the opportunity to bring fourth some blood came months ago he gladly offered to deliver. He also wanted to prove to himself that he was not just a spoiled kid who was handed everything he had.

Although he liked the special treatment, he got from his peers he always felt like it was not genuine. He despised people like Reggie. Athletic, sporty and tall it always seemed like they got what they want at his expense. This was his experience growing up. He was never the guy who got the girl. Even when he started to make a lot of money women seemed to always pick the other guy. When Mr Dean instructed him to befriend Reggie, he jumped at the opportunity. It was his form of payback.

To complete the hurumbo sacrifice they needed two bodies. One was the blood of a female representing the strength of the deity's feminine side and the other was to be a male with direct bloodlines to Cilocy. This was the difficult part as in previous years they had to travel out to Portugal to go and seek out a person. They would lure the unsuspecting victim with the promise of a high paying job and once the person arrived in the United Kingdom they would end up missing.

This was a risky and tasking method which they couldn't do all the time, but Mr Dean had stumbled upon an opportunity while speaking with one of his employees. He had lent him some money and he was struggling to pay back. Mr Dean would give loans to people in the community, but he was also known to be an enforcer when it came to collecting. His people would threaten those who struggled to payback the loans with inflated interest rates. To him this was a smart way to keep people under his jurisdiction.

Mr Dean helped one of his employees to buy a house. The employee happened to have Portuguese roots. He was struggling to pay the money back. Being from the same background as his boss he knew what would eventually happen so he offered to give some valuable information. He told him that his niece who lived in Leicester was a widow of a Cilocy member. It was known that he was poisoned back in Zimbabwe by the other members when he stopped them from coming to his store to gather as they had always done.

He converted to Christianity so they killed him. His wife and kids were now living in Leicester giving them the perfect opportunity to get a Male sacrifice with Cilocy blood ties. The Judas even had photos of his niece's two children Reggie and Esther. Chris volunteered to be involved in the meticulous planning of getting Reggie as their sacrifice so they carefully planned how they would keep him under their radar.

After doing some digging, they found out that Reggie worked at Pegasus Properties which presented a good opportunity for them to approach him. The plan was for Chris to befriend Reggie. When they watched his movements it was easy to see that Reggie had a string of women he entertained so it would be easier to entice him using a woman. Malantha knew what was going on and she never really got involved until she saw a picture of the Adonis of a man who was the target. She decided she wanted a piece of the action too and made it her mission to seduce him. Like a moth to flame, Reggie fell for the mysterious, wealthy, older lady.

He knew exactly what it was, just fun and nothing serious. To him she was just another rich lady with more time on her hands than sense. He had dealt with her type before. He caught her looking at him with lustful eyes at the shirt aisles in House of Fraser. After striking a flirtatious conversation she offered to pay for both his shirt and a suit to match. She was daring, he liked it so they ended up going to a wine bar and that same evening she invited him back to her mansion where they drank some more and had steamy sex.

That was the beginning of many nights like that. Chris made it a point to conveniently bump into Reggie at bars and restaurants he frequented until one day he invited him to go for a drink at the Crypt.

Reggie reminded him of the guys from his high school who always seemed to have all the women. Reggie was tall with an athletic build and an adventurous nature which women loved. Chris was short, a bit chubby and highly insecure. He hid his insecurities well just like the time he asked Reggie to help him get in shape and that they became gym buddies. Deep inside it crushed his ego and motivated him to follow through with the plan so he could get his own revenge. He also had a long-standing crush on Carmen.

Their two families were close so he hoped they would have something going on, but it never happened despite attempts from the both sides to make it happen. Marrying within the society was the norm, but Carmen did not want anything to do with Cilocy which caused a rift between herself and her parents.

Chris introduced Reggie to Carmen and Freya hoping that Reggie would fall for the curvy vibrant Freya. This would have made it easier for him to catch Reggie unaware in the hope that at some point they would go to Freya's apartment. He rented out his old apartment to Freya so he had a spare set of keys meaning he could gain entry at any time. He figured he would ambush Reggie at some point and with the help of other Kumoz subdue him when he was vulnerable. He had it all figured out except he didn't have a contingency plan when Reggie fell for Carmen instead.

This threw a wrench in his plans causing delays and pressure from the society. When the other sacrifice was due Chris decided to go for the easy option by suffocating Freya with a pillow while she was sleeping. They cut out her heart, put her body in the trunk and drove to Victoria Park where they dumped the body, which was found the next day. The full details of the homicide never went public because the police made sure of it under the instruction of the Chief who was a Cilocy member.

CHAPTER 11
Trust Nobody

Reggie had been staying at his mom's house for a couple of weeks recovering and clearing his mind. He was not taking calls and he had also been given some time off from work. His mind had been running through so many possible scenarios. He had told Carmen that he was spending quality time with family and that she probably needed to do the same. The truth is he felt conflicted about their relationship.

He did not know who to trust except his family. He started recollecting the time when he saw Chris dashing out of the Crypt soon after Mr Dean did and the dots started to connect. He figured Chris must have been working for Mr Dean and they must have been following his every move even before he got introduced to Carmen.

It hurt him to even imagine that Carmen was part of this, "how could she?" He thought maybe this is the reason she avoided talking about her parents. Carmen's last name was Rosario instead of Dean, maybe she lied to him to conceal the fact that she was a Dean. Everything started to make sense from the encounters with Malantha to the house purchase facilitated through him. The biggest question in his mind was why they were after him. This was more than just a husband seeking revenge for sleeping with his wife and daughter, there was definitely a lot more to it. Little things started to make sense like the fact that Carmen's watch was identical to the one Malantha and Mr Dean wore and he was sure Chris wore the same watch. Not only that, he was sure he had also seen it somewhere, but he couldn't figure out where that was.

It was Chris who had suggested and almost insisted they stay at Armathwaite Hall in Cumbria that weekend so he was the only one who knew. As much as he found it a hard pill to swallow it was quite obvious that he was the one following them in the black range rover the whole time.

Reggie and Esther sat at the dinner table. They were talking about childhood stories when Kainga brought the family photo album with pictures of family members and old houses they'd lived in. "Olhe aqui!" (Meaning look here) she said with a warm smile on her face walking towards with table with the thick photo album the same size as a laptop. "I can't believe you still have that," Reggie said smiling back while twisting his neck to look in his mother's direction.

"I'm pretty sure if this house ever got burnt down that would be the only thing she'd worry about," Esther said while moving the chair in front of her to make her way to the kitchen to make some drinks. She rolled her eyes playfully walking past Kainga who had placed the album on the table. Kainga always enjoyed having them both in the house and if she had it her way she wanted them to stay right there with her, but she knew it was impossible so she cherished times like these.

"I'll have a beer instead," Reggie yelled out to Esther after hearing the sound of the electric kettle boiling to make tea.

Kainga gave him the side eye and he said, "Only one beer won't hurt mom. Besides, I'm alright now," he added, gently rubbing his mom's arm as a gesture of reassurance.

They started going through the pictures starting with the black and white ones of Kainga and Reggie senior on their wedding day. Kainga's memories around their wedding was bitter sweet because back then interracial marriages were uncommon so their relationship was surrounded by a lot of politics. Times were different now, so Reggie and Esther were not trying to hear any of her stories which they had heard a thousand times before.

Reggie and Esther started making comments about their dress sense back then. Pastel sheath and swing dresses with low heel shoes. Their mother swore the fashion back then was a lot more sensible and their dad wore bell-bottomed pants with big-heeled shoes. In some pictures which looked like they were taken in the late 60s, he mainly wore single breasted sack jackets with narrow notch lapels.

This was almost consistent in all the images of their father who was very handsome with short back and side hairstyle with the side part.

Something caught Reggie's eye while going through the pictures. He noticed his dad wore the same wristwatch as the Deans. At first, he thought he was imagining things, but when he saw a close up photo of it in one of the photos, he was certain. Everything went on mute after that and he started to see that the situation was a lot more complicated than he thought.

"Are you sure you don't want to come with us honey? It might do you good getting out the house for a couple of hours," her mom said sounding concerned, but Carmen was in no mood to see people or be seen.

"I'll be fine here," she responded before her mother could say anything else.

"We love you baby," Mr Dean said holding the door for his wife to walk out the house so they could go out for lunch.

"Love you too," she said while waving goodbye to them both. Carmen had been living at her parent's new house receiving the best attention and care since leaving the hospital. Her parents made sure she had a nurse to look after her and the Chef made her anything she wanted to eat. It almost seemed like she was on vacation except it didn't feel that way.

When she observed the car leaving the mansion gates through the security monitors she poured herself a glass of cognac and started going up the grand stairs to her bedroom. Carmen had not told her parents that she got engaged for the simple fact that they would not approve of her fiancé.

She made it a point not to wear her ring in their presence to avoid suspicion. To her surprise they had asked questions about the whole incident, but they hadn't really asked for too much detail and she wondered why because they were the type to leave no stone unturned about anything.

Physically she felt like she was back to normal and all she wanted to do was be with Reggie, but he was acting a bit distant since the hospital. She thought the whole thing might have affected him more than she imagined so she was giving him some space. She so wanted to just leave the lonely mansion to be with her man, but she also felt like it was a good opportunity to patch things up with her parents and maybe just maybe introduce them to the man who stole her heart.

Even though she was raised in a family who practiced Cilocy she never did partake in any of the family's ideologies. It got worse when she started going to high school and started rebelling against her parents who she felt were controlling. She ran away on several occasions only returning when she ran out of money and as she grew older, her relationship with her parents got worse.

They would only allow her to date guys from a wealthy upbringing with similar values.

She preferred dating regular guys like her high school sweetheart Kurt who was the football captain, they were inseparable. One semester Kurt stopped coming to school and she didn't understand why he would just do that without warning.

He changed his number and his family moved to another city in a different county. It took her a while to get over her first love. Even after that her boyfriends seemed to go from hot to cold fairly quickly and she started to think there was something wrong with her. The one's that tended to stay were the arrogant rich boys ,, but she couldn't stand their attitudes and expectations of entitlement.

 A few years later, she bumped into Kurt while visiting a friend in Coventry, which is about 30miles away from Leicester. When she asked why he left without warning he told her that her family had threatened his family to move and insisted he stopped seeing her. He explained that the threats were malicious and because they had heard stories about her father's strong hand, they didn't take it lightly so they left.

Carmen confronted her parents and told them she would never forgive them, she packed her clothes and went and moved in with a friend till she found a place of her own. To sever ties with her parents Carmen changed her surname from Dean to Rosario. Since then their relationship became sketchy and close to non-existing.

That is until she met Reggie who was very close to his family and always talked about the importance of it. It made her want to reconcile with her family and the accident had made that possible. She wasn't quite sure why they hadn't questioned her to the third degree about Reggie. Part of her wanted to think that maybe they had changed now that she was a grown woman, but another part of her thought they hadn't changed one bit. She just thought they weren't concerned.

She had been in the new mansion for a while and hadn't really explored it. Her mother and father were out so she put her ring back on and started daydreaming. To get her mind off wanting to call Reggie she went back downstairs to refill her glass, but there was just a little amount of Cognac left. Both her parents were avid drinkers so in the first few days she had been there she had seen them going to the cellar enough times.

Carmen walked towards the kitchen were the cellar was, even with the scent of her beverage lingering on her she could still smell the sophisticated sultry note of vetiver from most of house. There was so much space especially for two people, but it didn't feel empty because there was so much to grab your attention from the high barrel-vaulted coffered ceilings, expensive artefacts and paintings, all too much to take in a day.

She pushed open the solid mahogany double doors, popped the light switch illuminating a spacious octagonal wine room. The rustic brick walls complimented the Brazilian walnut floor.

The shelving and display also made of mahogany wood lined from the floor all the way to the ceiling there must have been around one thousand bottles of wine. The way she was feeling wine wouldn't do the trick so she walked over to another section of the cellar where the spirits were kept.

 She grabbed the rope handle of the wooden cabinet with the see through glass, opened it and pulled out a bottle of aged Louis the 13th Remy Martin cognac. Her dad especially was a wine connoisseur and one of his hobbies was to bring an expensive bottle of wine from every country he travelled to. So it wasn't a surprise that the cellar would be this exquisite complete with a state of the art cooling system which kept the temperature at around 59 degrees. The temperature was controlled by a touch pad mounted on the wall next to the spirit cabinet.

The control pad looked like one of those security panels you would expect to see in sci-fi movies with different coloured neon light keys. On the pad there was a key with a little chandelier icon. When she touched it, the room lighting changed to a sensual red. She touched it several times and each time the lighting changed. She imagined having wild sex with Reggie in her parent's cellar. She played around with the other functions and apart from playing music and activating voice commands there wasn't much else.

As she walked back towards the double doors going past the hundreds of wine bottles, it caught her eye that one of the bottles of red wine was not actually a bottle. A person who is not as eagle eyed as she is would have walked right passed it as she nearly did. She thought it was strange, so she tried to pull the bottle out and she couldn't. It was almost glued on the shelving, but when she put a little effort with a slight counter clockwise twist the bottle shifted into gear and all of the sudden the room went dark which sent her in a panic.

The darkness did not last long because the shelves behind started to divide in two, sliding in opposite directions revealing a huge space which had dimmed lighting.

"The hell," she said to herself, if she wasn't in her parents' house she would have screamed her heart out. She almost dropped the Cognac bottle she had in her left hand, but as she advanced forward into the dim room, she instinctively swapped the bottle into her right hand.

She gripped the bottle tighter in case she had to swing it into someone or something. She felt like ice had replaced her spine when she saw staffs made of what seemed to be human bones with little crosses on the top all on the sides of the room around a sitting area.

The air was very supernatural, it made her feel an eerie discomfort. She knew her parents practiced Cilocy, but she was never around it enough to know the inner workings so she really wondered what took place when they all met in a room like this. Making sure not to touch or disturb anything she slowly walked to the front of the room and on a pedestal she saw what looked like blood stains and it gave her goose bumps when she imagined them to be real.

She actually let out a loud scream when she saw a human skull right next to a huge gold antique French style throne chair. Carmen lost grip of the cognac bottle she was holding and it smashed loud on the floor leaving a big mess.

"Argggggghh shit," she uttered knowing she had to clean it up herself even though there were helpers to do that, but she figured her parents would not have approved of her snooping around. She gasped, trying to calm herself down and control her breathing. She put her hand on her chest and patted gently to compose herself.

"Ok, ok, broom, I need to find a broom and clean up this mess," she muttered to herself knowing she had to do it fast before her parents got back. She started to look around hoping she would find some storage cabinets with cleaning stuff. She almost walked into the broken glass pieces on the floor because she was still in a bit of a panic. Carmen adjusted her hair and quickly ran out of the room into the cellar then into the kitchen where she bumped into one of the helpers.

"Hi, do you know where I can find a broom and mop? I made a small mess in the Cellar and I want to clean it up," she politely asked flashing a genuine smile.

"No don't worry I clean for you," she responded in an Eastern European accent, and before she could finish Carmen interrupted her, "It's ok; it's just a small mess. I can do it. Besides, I am not doing anything at all. It'll keep me busy."

"No problem. I left broom in the study," she said pointing towards the study, which Mr Dean used as his office.

It was downstairs on the other side past the living room and the sliding doors were slightly open so she went in and causally strolled to the corner where the broom was. She picked it up quickly and looked around to see if she could find anything else to help her clean that's when she saw a photo of Reggie on her father's desk. Carmen thought she was seeing things because she had been thinking about Reggie a lot so she thought this was some kind of optic illusion.

She picked it up and, indeed, it was Reggie in the picture. She started to wonder if her parents had already met him and if they were doing some kind of background checks on him. She thought maybe they may have seen him at the hospital. She definitely knew she did not have any photos of him on her so how on earth had the photograph ended up at her dad's desk? The only thing which made sense to her was they were going to find him and threaten him to leave her like they did with Kurt years back. Carmen felt the rush of emotions filled with resentment, hate and anger returning to her.

She thought to herself that she wasn't going to let them ruin the one thing which made her happy and that was her relationship with Reggie. She figured she would have to die first and she knew what she was up against, but she was not about to lie down and play dead. She went and slid the doors shut so no one could see her going through the papers on the desk and into the drawers which were not locked. A lot of it was just paperwork of miscellaneous stuff. Carmen did not know what exactly she was looking for.

Carmen carried on rummaging through the drawers of the resolute style desk in her father's office until she came across a brown envelope in the bottom drawer. It stood out because unlike the other drawers which had a mixture of paperwork and files this particular envelope was on its own. It must have been important. She was so fixated on it that she did not care to close the drawer.

Without thinking, she moved to the side of the table so she could get in a comfortable position to open the envelope with both hands. Carmen pulled up a black and white ten by six inch photograph of a man who had a strong resemblance to Reggie both in stature and features. She was sure this was a photo of his father. More so when she compared the image to Reggie's image which was already on the desk.

There was another photo of family members with the same man which she assumed were his wife and kids and this time she did not spend time analysing it. She just placed it on the side and kept emptying the contents of the envelope. What she saw next knocked every wisp of air from her lungs, she stood there struggling to inhale or exhale holding a picture of Freya in her hand.

Her bowels churned as she remembered some of the details of Freya's death, tears started flowing and she found herself fighting the sudden need to vomit with disgust, hate, and the implications which came with all this. She was still trembling and those salty drops falling from her chin were now drenching her top as she blacked out into oblivion of confusion and mixed emotions.

Somehow, she managed to calm herself down and get back to dealing with what she was potentially being confronted with. While putting the pictures back in the envelope the sparkle from the ring on her finger revived her spirits reminding her of the love of her life who was in grave danger.

Carmen ran out of her father's study with the envelope in hand and went straight up to her room to dial out for a taxi to come pick her up as soon as possible. Straight after she dialled Reggie's number which rang a couple of times before going to voicemail. "Please pick up Reggie, please pick up", she murmured to herself as she dialled the number once more, but it went to voicemail again after a couple of rings. She couldn't help wondering if something had happened to Reggie already, if "they" had got to him already. She pondered with the idea of calling the police, but she did not have any solid proof of what was going on and she also knew her parents had close ties with the authorities.

All these thoughts made her heart race, brain synapses firing like a hyped up internal aurora borealis. She felt like getting as far away from the mansion and her parents as possible so she grabbed her bag with her purse, stashed the brown envelope in it, threw on a jacket and dashed to the taxi which was now waiting outside. She hopped in the taxi like a fugitive on the run, gave the driver the address to Reggie's apartment and the taxi started to drive off.

CHAPTER 12
Lost Ones

"Pedro was one of our most loyal employees so we are still at a great loss Mrs Sercev. I know your family is at an even greater loss." He listened to the other person on the line for a moment then said, "well like I said earlier, the children's tuition will be taken care of up to university and his house is already paid for, if you need anything else don't hesitate to call me Mrs Sercev, please." He respectfully ended the conversation with Mrs Sercev who was mourning the death of her son Pedro a close friend of his.

Chris first met Pedro at a bar in Leicester city after he got into a brawl over a girl with a bunch of local guys. Pedro worked as a bouncer at the bar so he stepped in and stopped the guys from getting into it with Chris. They clicked ever since. Pedro was a tough guy with a tough image so Chris offered him a better paying job working for him and his family business. This included everything from collecting debts, being a personal bodyguard, a driver or doing anything the boss asked. Even though the two had a different upbringing they both felt like outcasts with Pedro being an immigrant from Bulgaria and Chris generally always having had a low self-esteem they developed a strong camaraderie.

There had been other soldiers who had worked for Chris and fallen victim to the type of work he was into. For him these were mere causalities of war so he did not lose sleep over them. In fact he barely remembered their names. When they set up on a mission to follow Reggie and Carmen to Wales they were more than prepared for every possibility except being hit by a truck while attempting to derail the car their target was in.

Pedro died at the same hospital he was in and it hit Chris hard. When he learned that Reggie and Carmen had made it almost unscathed it intensified his animosity towards Reggie and fuelled his lust to pursue him for horombo sacrifice.

He was running out of time and patience. He couldn't fathom the thought of potentially having to play the best friend role again. After all under the current circumstances he knew his cover could have been blown. It made him physically sick knowing that Reggie could outwit him even with the resources he had at his disposal.

Chris poured himself a glass of the amber liquid which glowed from the Waterford Lismore crystal decanter by the corner table in his condor apartment. Feeling a burn on his tongue and throat normally made him recoil, but the venom of his thoughts alone overpowered the strength of the single malt he was drinking.

As if the solutions to his problem lied in the whiskey he poured himself another, but before he could drink it his cell phone rang. When he looked at it the name "Carmen" was displayed so he hesitated to answer because he was not sure if Carmen knew that he was in fact the boogie man. The phone stopped ringing for a while then it started chiming again with the same name on the caller ID so he quickly gulped the whiskey he had poured, prepared himself for the worst case scenario and hit the accept button.

As soon as she realised Chris had picked up she burst out all her emotions. In a similar fashion to that of someone who has the duct tape over their mouth removed as they plead for their life to be saved. "They killed Freya, I know they did and they will kill Reggie Chris, they killed Freya!" she said in a total panic infused indignant uproar. "I don't know what to do?" she added in the same frantic manner. As she said all this Chris listened diligently and by this time he was now sitting on his Timothy Oulton sofa crossing his short chubby legs eyebrows extended. He obviously realised that Carmen hadn't caught on that he was involved so like a classically trained actor he got into character. "What,?, wait slow down Carmen you are not making sense right now, calm down okay, who is they and why do they want to kill Reggie?" he said trying his best to sound like he didn't know what she was saying.

He listened to her repeat the same statements evoking the same emotion that's when he interjected saying, "Okay! Carmen, listen lets figure this out together, you sound like you're in a car where are you going?"

She told him she was going to Reggie's house and she had been trying to reach him, but he wasn't picking up. Quick thinking Chris realised that this might have been the be opportunity he'd been waiting for so he came up with a plan to convince Carmen to do a detour to his house so they could figure things out together.

Possibly head out to Reggie's house together to minimise the chances of her being overpowered by whatever she would be confronted with. He communicated this to Carmen in a way that was as sincere as a kindergarten teacher. She helplessly agreed and instructed the taxi driver on the change of plans before she ended the call. After delivering what he thought was an Oscar worthy performance Chris immediately went to his phonebook section and started to call for reinforcements.

"Honey come down to the kitchen, we brought you some food, we got your favourite" Malantha hollered in her authoritative yet motherly voice. "Carmen, honey I got those prawns from Jimmy's on London road." She placed the paper bag with the food on the granite work top and proceeded to get a glass so she could fix herself a drink. When Mr Dean who was looking upstairs expecting her daughter to come down saw his wife getting the glass he knew what was coming next. He started making his way to the cellar to get a bottle for his wife.

Malantha chatty nature mostly irritated Mr Dean so he seldom anticipated anything which would potentially be a topic of argument. He noticed the double doors were ajar and the lights were on which was odd because he knew not to do that. It would affect the temperature of the cellar. The cellar felt colder than usual so he checked the temperature on the control pad and surely someone had messed with it. Apart from being a wine connoisseur, Mr Dean was also a perfectionist. The Cellar and much of the house was arranged to his specification, but he was particularly fond of this part of the house hence no one was ever allowed in there unless they were escorted by him.

Like magma in a volcano his blood was boiling as he built up anger. He twisted the lever on the shelving which was well disguised to look like the other wine bottles and walked straight to their worship room. It did not take him long to see the shattered pieces of glass and semi dried brown liquid on the floor, this confirmed the obvious fact that someone had been in there. "shit!"he said scanning the place to see if anything else had been broken or missing.

He marched back to the kitchen where Malantha was and she immediately could tell by his demeanour that something was wrong. "Where is your daughter?" he demanded. "I will go and get her?" she said calmly trying not to agitate him any further. Malantha started to walk up to the stairs when she saw the Eastern European helper and asked her where her daughter was. The helper told her that she had left in a taxi hours ago.

When she told her husband that their daughter was not in the house his chest tightened into a knot like a cramp as a quiet rage built up inside of him. Mr Dean was a man of few words whether he was in a good or bad mood. Those who knew him could normally judge his current mood by his body language. His body language was tense and his jaw clenched while he stormed off in huff, uttering under his breath and when he got to his study the door was already open. His attention was drawn to the desk which looked like a snowstorm went through it.

The bottom drawer was open and soon as he noticed the brown envelope was missing he focused his gaze at Malantha who stood by the study door in silent awe, too shocked to speak. Mr Dean pulled out his cell phone and dialled her daughter's number and she rejected the call twice. He put his phone back in his pocket and started to think about what she might have seen. This time around she had truly tried his patience.

CHAPTER 13
Gut Feels

Reggie had taken one of the pictures of his father from his mom's photo album collection. He was now determined to find out all he could about his father. His gut feeling told him that would be the best way to unravel the roots of what was going on.

He was still staying at his mother's house not only because of his mother's cooking, but also because kainga as Esther were the only people he truly trusted. He had never brought any of his co-workers or girlfriends to his mom's house. The only person who got close was Carmen, but he was glad he hadn't brought her there. At that moment he didn't know if Carmen was part of the plot or not. He was conflicted, but he thought to himself that if Carmen was truly involved she wouldn't have been in the car with him. Then again now that he realised that she was a Dean it was better to treat them all like enemies. As the saying goes, if it walks like a dog, barks like a dog and looks like a dog it must be a dog.

He noticed the vintage coins on is Westbury Grey table. The table looked smaller than usual. Looking around he could tell he was in his old room at their old house in Zimbabwe. That frowsty smell from the old furniture gave him pleasant nostalgia. He picked up the coins and walked to the door in front of him so he could go and give them to his father. The door was so little because he had grown so big he wouldn't have been able to go through.

He put the coins in his pockets and got on his knees so he could crawl and squeeze through the tiny door. The floor suddenly melted into a pool of blood. Reggie tried to lift himself off the ground to avoid the oozing gore of red which was fast inching out to every corner in the room, but his legs felt foreign and weakened. It felt like he'd been tranquilized.

All he seemed to manage was helpless movements from his limbs while he clawed into the cerise substance hoping to find something to hold on to. He screamed on top of his lungs, but only his mouth opened and nothing came out yet he didn't stop. He felt totally helpless as his whole body started being swallowed from beneath into a ghoulish abyss. The ordeal was worsened by echoic hubbub in the form of distorted radio waves, he held on to what felt like a hand which temporarily stopped him from being engulfed.

Indeed, it was a hand, a bloody hand for that matter, and in a random sequence more bloody hands started appearing from the surge of sticky blood. Grabbing every part of him and forcing him into the hole. The noises got louder and high pitched, it was a mixture of children and adult voices calling his name and telling him to save himself.

The hands slithered and transformed into serpents which coiled up on his body dragging him in. Reggie prepared to hold his breath before his head got submerged and through the tiny door on the other side was his mother sitting peacefully on a couch with her eyes closed hands on the bible. At that moment any hope he had dispersed and he decided what was going to be would be so he stopped fighting.

He felt another grip on his wrist. A much drier, firmer grip which felt familiar and when he looked at the hand he noticed the same watch with the cross emblem. When up he looked up he saw his father, in his youthful imposing form. Reggie called his father's name, but he did not say a word, he just completely pulled him out of the hole to where they were now standing face to face at the same height as if it was one man looking at his image in the mirror. With tears rolling from his eyes Reggie leaned forward to hug his dad, but he grabbed onto thin air and started falling into a pitch black pit.

A bright flash appeared and before he hit the ground his eyes snapped open. He was covered in a cold sweat, shaking and heart pounding. Reggie looked around the room suspicious and paranoid about what he had dreamt about. It felt so real so he got up shivering, rubbed his head and eyes to fully awaken. The darkness in the room made him yearn for light so he spread the curtains wide open to let the light in revealing the mundane morning activity of life in Coalville village.

That morning Reggie washed his face, brushed his teeth and composed himself so his mother and sister wouldn't notice that he was spooked. He normally got his mother to interpret his dreams, partly because he found it amusing and rather entertaining. That particular dream felt different and realistic in nature. Kainga and Esther had been excellent at aiding his recovery process, but he felt that telling them about his predicaments would have made them mollycoddle him. In his usual fashion he went to the kitchen where everyone usually congregated in the morning. He got involved in the small talk a little then he made his coffee and headed back to his room to send a couple of emails, that was how he politely excused himself.

Reggie cracked his lap top open and powered it up. He got his father's photo out the drawer and fixed his eyes on the watch. He logged in and went onto Google search to type in "watches with a cross logo." As he expected the results came back with over twenty eight thousand hits. This wasn't going to be easy.

From the little he knew it was evident the people involved went to great lengths to keep their intentions and operations discreet. He started paying extra attention to the images which had the closest resemblances to the one in the photo. He was prepared to move heaven and earth so he got comfortable and carried on looking page by page.

After hours of painstaking comparisons and due diligence he narrowed it down to an image of a Vacheron Constantine Swiss watch. Reggie zoomed in on the image of watch and held his Fathers picture next to it and it was a perfect match. This reinvigorated his curiosity levels so he went on the Vacheron Constantine website and looked at their vintage collection. The watch his father wore in the picture was identical to the range named 'les collectionneurs' complete with the leather straps.

The watches were originally designed by Jean-Marc Vacheron over 260 years ago in 1755. The timepieces were definitely the labour of unique craftsmanship with extraordinary aesthetics. Famous people like Marlon Brando and his majesty king Farouk I of Egypt were amongst the few elite who had these pieces.

Further digging on Jean-Marc Vacheron himself revealed that he perfected his unique watch making skills in Switzerland however, his father was Portuguese. Learning that fact alone was the first real indication that he was onto something because Reggie's father was of Portuguese origin. Reggie also discovered that Jean had connections with King Manuel I and the Portuguese Armada. Growing up in the Portuguese community there was always a form of underlying fear for families who had close ties with King Maunel I based on how he and his merciless henchmen dealt with those who defied him.

Reggie's uncle once told them about an alleged incident where a group of men were hung by large metal hooks attached to ropes which were slung over a roof girder allowing the bleeding victims to be hoisted off the ground. Suspended only by their skin they bled and passed out from the gruesome pain until they died. Reggie was highly sceptical about the accuracy of these tales. He likened them to the embellished folk tales he read about as a child. Never the less the fact was his life was in danger and he needed to do something about if fast.

For the next four days Reggie left no stone unturned. He quickly learnt that there were no local stores selling the watches. The nearest store was forty three miles away in the city of Birmingham in the west midlands. The store staff were pleasant enough when he called and booked an appointment to look at their collection for a possible purchase. He caught the train to Birmingham's new street station then he got into a taxi to the store located within the jewellery quarter. The store was very elegant, not as big as he expected, but the sparkling glass shelves and counters gave the feeling of extra space.

There were different sections with all types of jewellery and then there was a section for watches. He was greeted by a member of staff who also offered him a drink and sat him down while he browsed through the catalogue provided. Moments later a middle aged man who introduced himself as Steve came and set down opposite Reggie and they started talking about watches.

Steve who had a rather monotonous voice showed him different expensive time pieces. He was very patient with Reggie who was intentionally being indecisive. Somewhere in the middle of the page, he saw a Vacheron watch and pointed to Steve showing him that he was interested in that particular one. Steve mentioned they didn't have the watches in stock, but they had other ones which were better. Reggie insisted on that one and nothing else.

Steve said, "We have a special waiting list for that watch sir, we are currently not taking any orders at all" in the same monotonous voice which was becoming more and more annoying by the second. Steve's body language had all the signs of a person telling lies so Reggie decided to up the ante and said, "I am a friend of the Deans" in a confident tone. The manager immediately got up and said, "Please can you exit the store sir." He said that with such seriousness and conviction that the rest of the staff immediately glared at Reggie as if he was the bearer of bad news.

Steve commanded the guy who initially greeted Reggie to guide him to the door. The guy who wasn't as friendly as before gestured for Reggie to walk in his direction towards the door. Knowing that places like this were quick to call security or even police Reggie complied. The tension was palpable and he had definitely overstayed his welcome, but before he pushed the glass doors open he felt a note being slid into his pocket. Without saying a word he turned his head and the guy who had escorted him to the door gestured with his eyes and head for Reggie to hurry on out. He flagged down a taxi and got driven to the station back to Leicester and not once did he try to read the note until he got home.

The note read, "Call Aleixo, watch your back."

There was a number written on it. That night Reggie didn't sleep at all. He tossed and turned all night, thinking about what transpired at the watch store and wondering what he would find out next, especially if he called the number. He wasn't even sure if calling the number was a good idea. After all how could he trust the person who gave him the note? He had no way of knowing if it was a set up or not so all these thoughts made him restless and anxious. After putting everything into consideration he figured what's the worst that could happen.

There had already been an attempt on his life so stopping now would not slow these people down. By midday the next day, Reggie had summoned up enough courage to make the call. When he made the call the person on the other line said he'd been waiting for his call and gave him a time and place to meet. He did not say much and his words just tumbled slowly and cautiously out his mouth, each one wrapped in a heavy voice. So much that Reggie knew not to ask any questions even after knowing that he had to go to London to meet him the next day.

When the loud announcement came through the train intercom telling passengers that they were now arriving at St Pancreas station, people started reaching for their luggage and belongings. It was the fifth time he was thinking of turning back since boarding the train. He felt a weird combo of anxiety and fear causing his bladder to itch with the feeling of urine about to force itself out. He begged for forgiveness as he shuffled past the standing passengers lurching towards the restroom.

He locked the door behind him and soon as he was in there his urge to urinate was gone, so instead he washed his face with the trickling water from the faucet. He remembered his cadet training days when he learned controlled breathing techniques to calm his nerves. His short session was ended by the train's halt and the stampede of passengers disembarking. The intercom dinged again followed by a soothing voice, "Thank you for travelling with East Midlands Railway. Enjoy the rest of your journey."

Reggie had no luggage so he unlocked the door and joined the line of people who were pouring out from the cabin and walking onto the platform towards the exit gates. His legs felt wooden and stiff. He struggled to bend his knees properly so he waddled along with the sea of people who were holding their tickets to swipe through the gates. He got so anxious that he bumped into the lady in front of him, she apologised instead and he just nodded in acknowledgement, unwilling to risk speaking.

The woman allowed him to get in front of her which on a normal day he wouldn't have allowed. He was certainly not himself that day. He exited through the disabled wheelchair gate without swiping his ticket.

Reggie paid little attention to the majestic historical architecture of the Barlow shed above him. It span an amazing 240 feet, made of glass and steel to provide natural light. It also gave a unique contrast to the brick of the Midland Grand hotel which was built in the muscular years of Gothic Revival. The precise instructions from Aleixo needed him to take the escalator down to the ground floor. He stood on right hand of the escalator so he wouldn't distract people who were in hurry to go down.

As the escalator descended, he felt trickles of sweat streaks from his armpits flowing down his abdominal obliques and into his jeans. His right foot touched the ground first then his left followed hesitantly with a slight push from the escalator step and instantly he felt like he was being watched. Again according to precise instructions he looked on his right and saw a big blue sign written "information" on it so he started walking in that direction until he actually walked past the information desk. The public phones were on his left next to the ticketing booth and there was a small crowd in front of it. Slightly separated from the crowd there was a man wearing a black button down shirt with a brown jacket, some blue jeans and brown shoes. He noticed these items of clothing because that's what Aleixo said he'd be wearing. His hair was curly and mostly grey. He looked about 5 feet 9 with a chevron moustache. He also wore aviator style sunglasses with a heavy tint.

At that point, Reggie was totally unaware of his body movements as he approached the stranger. When he got close enough to speak to the guy, he asked "are you Aleixo?" sounding unsure and before he could finish the stranger said, "Just keep walking and follow me," in a familiar heavy voice.

Reggie followed the guy who glided along with ease like a waiter in a crowded restaurant, unbothered and not looking back to check if Reggie was there. They walked all the way to Pancras square and by then he was feeling more comfortable even though Aleixo hadn't said a word. They sat on the chairs next to the Caithness stone water feature. The water cascaded downhill on the different levels in an intricate movement and made a loud, but infectious sound.

"You're a chip off the old block", Aleixo said calmly, leaning back slowly in his chair.

"You look just like your father Reggie, I knew him well."

"I knew this day would come, you are in great danger son, and you have no idea who you are dealing with" he said.

"The one's before you, your grandfather, your father and you are from a bloodline of Cilocs."

Reggie, who hadn't said a word, leaned forward so he could catch every word. Aleixo told Reggie that Cilocy was something you were born into especially back home in Portugal and there was no way out. Families who were Cilocs or Kumoz which is what they called themselves, had vast wealth and influence, but there were many sacrifices which needed to be done to keep the Gorah happy.

"You can't escape it, they always find you, and it's in your blood," he explained. He was referring to the Gorah, which he described as the deity that all sacrifices are made to. He described other yearly esoteric rituals made to keep the deity satisfied with such ease like a psychopath being interviewed.

Aleixo explained how Reggie's father's decision to convert to Christianity got him killed. They gave his blood to the Gorah, as it requires pure blood in a ritual called *horombo*. Pure blood is blood that comes from a person within the bloodline. Reggie's whole body was tensed up as he tried the fathom all this.

"Even I can sense your fear, son you better throw that fear right out your soul because these people and the Gorah feed off fear, you hear me son?"

Reggie nodded while swallowing his own saliva to moisten his dry mouth and finally finding the strength to speak.

"How did you find me?" he asked with a drop of bravery in his tone.

"These creatures are like snakes who don't require love to raise their mammals, there are everywhere."

"Word travels fast in our world Reggie, I am a Kumoz too, part of this bloodline and I heard that you were being hunted down for the next horombo."

"I made a promise to your father to protect you as a favour he did for my family years ago."

"He smuggled my family to Zimbabwe to escape the civil unrest in Mozambique."

Aleixo took his glasses off and looked at Reggie with his good eye that was watery black. It was like a creature that spent its life in perpetual shadows. It was an intense stare as if he was looking into his soul. His other eye was missing and you could slightly see the red inside of the socket, which was an unsettling.

"Do you understand what I'm saying son, these people don't play by the same rule book as the rest of society."

"They win all the time Reggie, all the time you know why? Because they have no morals or restraints, they are wolves, but we don't have to be sheep we can be the lions."

"To kill the snake you have to kill the head, and you are closer to the head, that is Mr Dean."

"We should go now because they watch everything, listen son, listen carefully," he said grabbing Reggie's hand with his right revealing his Vacheron watch.

"I will call you and give you more details on how to get to Mr Dean..."

Just before he could finish the sentence, there was a subtle "whock" sound, and within seconds, a bullet had punched a hole on Aleixo's neck. The hole filled with blood and gushed out causing him to fall to ground. Reggie knelt down for cover, scared to death, heart pounding, and looking in the direction where the shot came from.

All pandemonium broke loose across the square as people ran and scattered on either directions of the water feature. Reggie's first instinct was to get away from Aleixo because whoever shot him must have been looking to shoot him too.

The only reason he didn't was his back was against the Caithness stonewall, leaving him vulnerable in the front. He watched a pool of blood forming around Aleixo who was muttering "Corre, corre" which means run until he choked to death on his own blood. Aware of the imminent danger Reggie's senses sharpened with adrenalin and he took off in the opposite direction to where the shot came from.

He blended into the crowds of people who scrambled disorderly for the nearest exits running past the armed police who were now charging to the scene. There was commotion in the entire station. Sirens were sounding and sections close to the square were cordoned off. The station workers were trying their best to keep the people calm

while putting safety measures in place. Reggie decided to go to the coach section instead because he figured it would be safer for him to take the coach back to Leicester. There were less people on a coach so he figured it would allow for better surveillance of the people boarding and disembarking. He was not even sure what a Cilocy member would look like so throughout the ordeal everyone he encountered looked suspicious.

He paid for his ticket and sat at the back of the coach for a better vantage point of everyone. The pounding in his chest decelerated as the coach pulled further away from the station. An hour later, the passengers on the coach were a general mix of some who were tired, bored, sleeping and others were indifferent. It was a much slower form of transportation and even though there were no road works on the M1, it took what seemed like forever to get to Luton station. This would have been the only stop before reaching his destination.

Though fatigued, Reggie was awake. Even without closing his eyes, he could see images of Aleixo's face bleeding. In a weird twisted way, the whole ordeal played out slowly in his head with muted dialogue. His dad's face flashed in his mind as the good and bad memories oscillated. Days when the family was still complete and the good old memories played like ripples in a pond after a stone had been thrown in. They slowly faded and dissolved, but the conversation with Aleixo remained fresh.

It kept echoing louder and louder forcing him to think about what he was going to do when he arrived in Leicester. Reggie looked on his phone which he hadn't checked for much of the day. There were several missed calls from Carmen.

He knew he needed her to be able to get to Mr Dean whether she was involved or not. He just didn't know how the conversation would go. Carmen had left a voice message so he listened to it. Hearing Carmen's voice made him realise that he still had feelings for her however, she sounded like she was in a panic.

"Reggie! Babe please call me back as soon as you get this."

"you are in danger please call me back when you get this, I am going to Chris's house at the moment so meet me there."

"Babe please call me back to say you are ok. I love you."

Reggie quickly dialled Carmen's number and it started to ring.

CHAPTER 14
Horombo

Chris's penthouse was located on the top floor at The Wullcumb opposite high cross on Vaughan way in Leicester city centre. From the balcony, it gave you a beautiful bird's eye view of the city. It had a private lift, large floor area, high vaulted ceilings, swimming pool and Jacuzzi.

The plush landscaping and endless luxury features of the dwelling drew women in like a moth to flame. He was boastful of the fact that he'd had many parties there and many drug and alcohol-fuelled orgies than he could remember. Things like that made him feel invincible and powerful.

He pushed the button, which authorised the lift to come up, and when his guests came to the door, they greeted each other the Kumoz way. He fixed them a drink and they started discussing what to do before Carmen arrived. The three guys were no rookies so it did not take long for them to understand what their respective roles were. Half an hour later, the elevator alert rang again and it was Carmen who had arrived.

The lift doors slid shut behind her, and the lift started to ascend up. The elevator had white marble walls, a red carpet and a gold handrail with no buttons to press like the public ones. It glided up gracefully past the many floors in the building making everything below it look like shrunk miniature boxes. Carmen knew she didn't look her best so it was a blessing that there was no mirror. She stood there with her bag worn over one shoulder.

Holding it close to her body and in the other arm, she had her cell phone. Carmen was more the outdoor loving country living type so she was unmoved by the all the opulence. All she could think about was Reggie, tapping her feet impatiently waiting for the doors to separate she was relieved when she finally reached the 10th floor. Carmen damn near squeezed out before the doors were fully opened and headed straight to the door where Chris was waiting to let her in.

Her eyes filled with tears of relief when she saw Chris and she hugged him, "he's not picking up

Chris, I think my parents have something to do with Freya's death, I'll explain, but first let's go and get Reggie"! She said in a broken voice filled with emotion. He hugged her back with deceit that could put Judas to shame and said, "Don't worry Carmen, sit down for a minute and calm down."

He led her to the stool by the bar section.

"I know you are worried about Reggie, I can tell you he'll be just fine," Chris muttered, revealing a crooked little smile.

All Carmen heard was the Reggie was fine part, so she stood up and said, "Have you spoken to him? Is he on his way?"

She asked, with a twinkle of hope in her tear-filled eyes. She asked the question twice, but Chris acted like he didn't comprehend what she was asking. He casually paced back to the door and locked it. He turned around and looked at Carmen who was clueless as to what was going on and said, "All I can tell you is Reggie is in big trouble."

The 3 men appeared out from a different door opposite the bar which caused Carmen to take a few uncalculated steps backwards knocking the stool right over.

"Who the fuck are they Chris? Where is Reggie?" pointing at the men and looking at Chris at the same time.

"You know what Carmen, that's always been your problem. You are too fucking spoiled, you expect people to always dance to your tune."

"Well this is my party, why don't you just shut the hell up and listen for a change?" He ordered with an evil gleam in his eyes.

She thought to scream, but based on the set up of the penthouses she figured no one would hear. She looked at her bag where her cell phone and jacket was. It was way on the other side close to Chris so she wasn't going to take the chance. Two of the men flanked her and the other guy was behind her. Chris was at the front. A shudder ran through her with the sudden realisation that she was trapped. Instantly the two men pounced and grabbed her by the arms to subdue her.

She involuntarily let out a rage-full scream that paralysed everyone's hearing. There were no holds barred kicking, biting and head butting trying to break free and make a run for it. The third man grabbed both her feet to stop her from jerking all over and they restrained her. They tied her to a Hemingway cane back dining chair they had prepared, but she was still forcing and fighting being hysterical.

Chris was growing impatient of both the men taking long to shut her up. His inner countdown had reached its limit so he walked to the chair. He loosed the bit of rope that was running below her breasts and placed it on the neck.

He dropped it over her shoulder and pulled it in a jerking motion. She stopped fighting instantly as the rope tightened on her neck and a small whimper escaped. Chris tied the rope on the chair leg and instructed one of the guys to pull it tighter when she started making noises.

He stood in front of her and bent over so he could make eye contact.
"What do you want Chris and what have you done with Reggie?" she hissed petrified trying to avoid his evil gaze. He ran his chubby hand on her lycra clad hip slowly and creepy. Then he started to rub her thigh and she winced. The guy pulled the rope tighter forcing her to stop. She couldn't imagine that the man her fiancé once called a

friend was morally capable of doing this, but for Chris morals were like infra-red beams in jewellery stores, invisible until crossed.

He stroked her until he was close enough to touch her nipples and she squeezed her eyes shut not knowing whether he was going to rape her or kill her.

She felt his breath on her cheek and her legs started to tremble mercilessly, he said in a low, but deliberate tone, "If you do as I say you will survive, but if you fuck with me you will end up like your little friend Freya, okay?"

There was a pause, she gulped and swallowed followed by a slow nod.

The upper corner of the brown envelope was poking out from her bag. Chris moved the jacket on top to the side and fished the envelope out. He pulled out the photos of Reggie's dad and Freya's and they did not grab his attention so he flipped the bag upside down on the bar counter and the contents spattered out. Chris didn't pay no mind to the miscellaneous personal items which were spread out disorderly, his eyes shifted to the iPhone which was closest to him. He picked it up and tapped the screen which lit up revealing a picture of Carmen and Reggie kissing as the screensaver.

Chris brazenly laughed holding the phone and walked back towards the chair, "Look at you two lovebirds. What the fuck did you expect from your Mr Hots here huh? A fairy-tale romance? Well you know your family Carmen, seems like your Mr Hots picked the wrong fucking girl this time."

He instructed her to unlock her phone and call Reggie and she reluctantly obliged. Reggie picked up after the first ring and heard a familiar voice, but it wasn't his fiancé, it was Chris instead.

"Hi Reggie, it's been a while I know you are probably wondering why I'm on Carmen's phone, but I promise you my dear friend. You will find out pretty soon."

Chris could almost feel the rage coming through the earpiece of the phone as Reggie asked to speak to Carmen.

"Calm the fuck down big boy, you are not in a position to be making demands right now, your girlfriend's fine, for now, maybe if you play nice I might let you speak to her."

Seething inside from the betrayal Reggie had no choice, but to comply with Chris's demands so he listened while Chris gave him instructions on what he needed to do. He was told to come to the address on his own, he was told that if he alerted the authorities Carmen would die and so would his mother and sister.

The call ended abruptly.

Reggie was already at the station so his instinct told him to head out to Coalville to his mother and sister. He called them first and they seemed fine and unassuming which made him feel relieved. His relief was short lived when the radio station in the taxi started talking about the incident at St Pancreas station. Reggie's life had literally turned into an unbelievable and unimaginable saga.

Reggie's mind was all over the place, he didn't know where to start. He felt like he needed help to try and figure everything out, but he couldn't trust anyone. He also feared the possibility of whomever he'd confide in turning up dead. He knew no one had ever been to his mother's house, but then he remembered Esther saying they had met the Deans at the hospital. He just hoped they hadn't given him their address.

There were a few days left before Horombo and they hadn't got the sacrifice yet so everyone was in a panic. Mr Dean was growing impatient of Chris's effort to deliver and he had made it clear in a couple of conversations they had. Chris had put together a new plan. The problem was his bargaining chip was Carmen. He knew Reggie would definitely show up however, he didn't know how Mr Dean would react knowing that they used his daughter. So Chris was faced with a dilemma.

The plan was when Reggie showed up to get Carmen they would also hold him hostage. This meant they would have to release Carmen. Releasing Carmen meant she would end up telling her father how they tied her up and forced her hand. He concluded that it would be beneficial to kill Carmen and make it look like Reggie did it. That way he would have killed two birds with one stone.

Mr Dean had exhausted all the ways of trying to contact her daughter. Her phone was not being answered and they really didn't know any of her friends which made it more difficult. In the end he told Malantha to keep trying to finding her. They contacted their friends in the local police to help.

The information she had was compromising and capable of ruining everything if it fell into the wrong hands. Mr Dean locked the door to his study and sat in his chair behind the resolute style desk pondering about solutions. His study was full of ancient books and some of them were collector's items. The desk which was in front of him was designed to replicate the one in the white house, but his had a secret compartment.

On one of the pilasters on the table the wooden pieces slid out to reveal a vertical hiding spot. Mr Dean put his finger in the opening and pushed a button which released a catch on the book shelves and a surveillance screen appeared. He was the only one in the house who knew about this, but he never felt the need to use it until now. Ever since the Crypt was compromised they held their meetings at the new house, but he still had old footage from the old house on an old drive. He sat there holding a small remote, fast forwarding footage on the various screens.

A lot of it was just stagnant especially in the rooms and areas he didn't expect workers to be in. The current mansion was big and modern, but the old one was even bigger. When they had 20 plus guests it still felt empty, that's what he missed. Being able to get privacy all the time. To break the monotony he pinched the piece of fabric near the cuff of his shirt and rubbed it back and forth between his fingers.

An image of a tall man appeared on one of the outside cameras. At first Mr Dean thought he could have been a delivery guy or some sort of sales person. He fast forwarded the footage as he had been doing with the rest, which clearly showed visitors turning back at the door. To his surprise the inside camera showed the man entering the house. The CCTV in the old house was the sophisticated type with small cameras disguised as screws or chandelier attachments. He watched as the man went upstairs.

His face fell faster than a corpse in cement boots when he zoomed in on the image and realised it was actually Reggie in his house. His mouth hung with lips slightly parted and his eyes were as wide as they could stretch. Mr Dean checked the date and time stamp on the right hand corner of the screen and quickly realised this had happened on the time he was away on business.

According to his movements Reggie seemed acquainted. It didn't take long for Mr Dean to see his wife, Malantha in all her naked glory walking up to Reggie. His brain cogs couldn't turn fast enough to take in the information from his widened eyes. The two naked bodies writhed on the bed in an embrace that made them oblivious to everything except their mutual ecstasy. The scene was unbelievable, shocking, and it sent his mind reeling unable to comprehend or process the images before him. He looked away, then looked back to see if it was still there. It was. Mr Dean did not watch anymore of it, he had seen enough and now his face was stuck in an incredulous expression and an unblinking stare.

Any man's world would have been totally crushed by something like this, but Mr Dean was not like any other man. He was the leader of Cilocy and the only one capable of summoning the Gorah. This powerful position gave him access to unimaginable resources. It did not take him long to decide that he was going to use his influence to make Malantha pay for this absurdity. The priority for him was to find Reggie since horombo was fast approaching and to also make sure his daughter had not showed what she had to anyone.

CHAPTER 15
Avalanche of Fear

Soon as the man got in the car he extended his hands to greet the driver. He already knew who was in the car because there weren't too many people in town who drove a Rolls Royce.

"I appreciate you agreeing to meet me at a moment's notice, how's the family doing?" "Family is doing, real good, after everything you have done and continue to do for us it's the least I can do."

"Like I said before I will always be at your service, just tell me what you need."

He noticed there were two men sat in the back, but that didn't surprise him for he knew Mr Dean always travelled with other people. Also this was not the first time they had met in that type of setting so he felt at ease. To him Mr Dean was most generous to him. Not only did he provide him with a job, but he always loaned him money when hard times hit. There were times he couldn't pay on time so he would do little favours for him. They had a similar Portuguese upbringing so he knew about Mr Dean's affiliations and connections.

For those reasons he knew not to cross him. He had heard through the grapevine about the repercussions of crossing him. So when he failed to pay back a loan toward purchasing a house he decided to give Mr Dean Information that was potentially worth more. He was the one who put Reggie on Mr Dean's radar because Kainga was his niece so he knew all the intricate details of the family. When the information proved fruitful his debt was wiped off. After that he'd met with Mr Dean on several occasions and managed to make himself some money at the same time. Which is why he didn't hesitate meeting him under these circumstances. He expected a ward of cash for another favour.

"Like I said Joao, I know you are a family man so thank you for coming, you have been of great assistance to our organisation, thank you."

"I just need one more favour and that will be all. I got this money for you", he said casually showing him an envelope with neatly packed twenty pound notes.

Joao played it cool and acted like money was not his motivation. He just nodded and did not interrupt while the man spoke. "I understand Reggie is at his mother's somewhere in Coalville, all I need from you is their address. Do you have it?" Joao gladly gave the new address, but thought it was odd that they came all that way just for that. To make it worth the payment he also gave directions on how to get there.

Mr Dean handed him the envelope and he quickly stashed it in his jacket pocket.

"By the way Joao, did you tell anyone that you were meeting me here?"

"Oh no, not at all, as usual I told the wife that I was going to meet a friend for a couple of drinks, that's why I caught the bus."

"Good man, well that'll be all."

"Pass my greetings to the family," Joao said while grabbing the door with his left hand.

The door did not open so he flicked the handle again with a lot more force and still the door stayed shut. With his body leaning towards the door, Joao turned his head to look at Mr Dean. He expected him to click some special button somewhere in the luxury vehicle and release the door however; the look on Mr Dean's face was filled with vileness.

"What's going on?" he asked, trying to conceal the avalanche of fear which was taking over. Using his eyes only, Mr Dean nonchalantly signalled the guys in the back seat and within seconds one of them pounced on Joao like a tiger does on its prey.

He wrapped a scarf around Joao's neck and started yanking. Joao fell back in the seat with both hands on the scarf trying to loosen it, but he struggled against the firm grip. There was some struggle as he dug his fingernails into the guy's wrists, trying to dislodge him. The grip was too strong to wriggle out of. This went on for what seemed like over five minutes. He gulped and gasped for breath, legs went from kicking to twitching.

Meanwhile, Mr Dean sat in the driver's seat looking the opposite way outside through the window as if he was listening to classical music. His face started to turn into a sickening colour and his eyes started to close in on him. Mr Dean only looked when Joao's hands fell to his side and all the energy escaped him. The guy in the back seat tugged on the scarf a few times just to make sure he'd finished the job. By the time, he stopped squeezing Joao was motionless, head slumped with his mouth open.

They strapped his motionless body into the seat to make it look like he was asleep and drove off from the secluded spot in Beaumont leys. They headed for the A46 towards Loughborough straight on to the A6 for six miles until they got to the river Soar. They emptied his pockets and took the money he had stashed in his jacket. They tied a rock onto his body to prevent it from floating before throwing it into the river. Mr Dean did not part-take in any of the handy work. He watched on as his two guys did all the dirty work when he was satisfied they drove back to the city.

Reggie got home in a panic, went straight to his room to start working on how he was going to possibly put an end to all this. The people he cared for the most were alive and well for now and he wanted to keep it that way. He still cared for Carmen even though he was not sure about her allegiances. Every time he thought about her his mind seemed to go back to the conversation they had on the boat at Bassenwaithe Lake when he proposed.

Something kept telling him that the tears of joy from Carmen that day were genuine. They did not look like the tears of a conniving, self- serving person. The Carmen he knew was loving and compassionate. The vitriol towards her had been reduced since the call from Chris, but he wasn't going to be unprepared this time. Especially after what he had witnessed first-hand with Aleixo.

Reggie was still in contact with some of the guys from his Cadet days. He contacted two of them and expressed his need to acquire weapons for protection. He met with two of the guys at a nearby pub. The guys were ex-military and they had a reputation for being good on their word and being honourable. They ran a successful private investigations company and provided security for high profile people. Reggie knew he needed to be honest with them from the beginning.

They were the only people he knew who had the right skill set required to handle Mr Dean and his crew. They sat in the corner of the pub and discussed everything about Reggie's predicament. Reggie told them everything about how he first met Mr Dean, Malantha and Carmen. All he knew about Mr Dean's affiliations and capabilities was laid out and they started setting up an intricate plot. It was agreed that the first mission was to go to Chris's apartment to rescue Carmen as soon as possible.

The three men walked to the grey Ford Ranger truck which was parked conveniently to give a 360 degree view of who would enter and exit the vicinity. In the car they had an array of weapons and ammunition. From sniper rifles to semi-automatic-pistols and revolvers stashed in a duffel bag. Reggie occasionally handled weapons at different gun ranges as a way of keeping himself sharp. He seldom used rifles so he naturally gravitated towards the revolvers he got shown.

He picked up a Llama 380 which he recognised from the distinct logo engraved on the handle. The knurled grip felt at home in his palm and it felt small enough to conceal. He opted for the ankle holster in case he got patted down. They had already looked at how Chris's penthouse building was laid out so they went through their respective positions and roles for the rescue mission.

Reggie returned to his mother's house just before it got dark. He didn't want to draw attention in the small village street so when he got dropped off by his friends he scuttled to the door. The first thing he noticed was the blinds were shut which was unusual because there was still daylight. He thought nothing of it and took his keys out of his pocket.

A black back pack slung over one shoulder he pushed the key in and the door just opened. This was odd because the door always stayed locked. The worry quickly grew into something more sinister when he stepped onto some shattered glass across the wooden floor. The glass was from a picture frame on a small table close the door. Judging from the way it landed it was clear that it was knocked down by someone on their way out.

His mother or sister would have cleaned that up even if it meant being late for anything. When he called out and nobody answered a river of chills swept through his spine. He was startled by the encompassing fear that seemed to blanket him.

The entire house had been ransacked and everything was upside down. His room in particular had all the drawers open and paper strewn about. Both Kainga's and Esther's phone were going to voicemail and he feared the worst might have happened till he saw a note stuck on the fridge which read. "I have your mother and sister, do not do anything stupid or I will kill them." He imagined what had taken place and how traumatizing it must have been for his mom and sister. It made him feel sick to the stomach to think that all his loved ones had been taken because of him.

Feeling overwhelmed with anger and vengeance Reggie screamed, repeatedly bashing his fists against the wall. He started to lose control of himself. The fury was boiling up inside of him and he was pacing up and down the room with the loaded revolver in his hand. At that moment there was no doubt in Reggie's mind that he was capable of killing. While frantically pacing in the living room he picked up the bible which was tossed next to Esther's Yamaha keyboard. Bible in his left hand, gun in the other he stood by the wall deflated in tears.

He slid down the wall crying, until he was seated on the floor. Reggie placed the gun next to him and started shuffling the bible's pages to Ephesians 5:19. It was one of his mother's favourite verses and they were always made to read it out loud. "Speaking to another with psalms, hymns, and songs of the spirit. Sing and make music from your heart to the Lord," saying that several times brought calmness to his spirit.

Reggie pulled himself together and tidied up the mess in the house as best as he could. Just like Aleixo said, these people had no souls and were willing to do anything. He took solace in knowing that he was the one they really wanted, so in some ways killing his loved ones wouldn't give them what they wanted for the sacrifice. There was a lot at stake and being strong was the only option he had. He remained steadfast in his belief that their plan with the guys was the right thing. To spark a little optimism Reggie booked one way tickets to Atlanta. When this was all over he wanted them to go as far away as possible and start over.

CHAPTER 16
Right Under My Nose

"You ungrateful bitch, so you just bring random men in my house and fuck them in our bed now?"

"What does this look like to you huh! Some cheap ass hotel?"

"What are you talking about? Come down and stop all this yelling," Malantha responded nonchalantly.

"How long have you been sleeping with Reggie?"

She was caught unawares, so her response was delayed.

"What do you mean?" Mr Dean grabbed her by the hand tightly and marched her to the study saying "you must think I'm fucking stupid, I said how long have you been fucking Reggie?"

He had the footage paused on the screen which Malantha had no idea existed until that moment. Her arm right above the elbow was bruised from being held so tight. She thought not to say anything until she saw the full recording. Five seconds into the video her jaw dropped open and the usual cockiness she always carried escaped from her.

The evidence was pretty damning. It was almost like the confrontation stage of the popular TV series Cheaters except the potential consequences for Malantha would be a lot worse. "Oh so all of a sudden you can't speak huh!" He said with his arms crossed over his chest like a warriors shield. She was totally caught off guard and she still had no words to say. She just stood there like a mannequin, silent, starring at the floor unable to admit the truth.

"You had him under my nose the whole time we were trying to find him and you knew where he was."

"You are lucky I have a lot on my plate right now, trust me I am going to deal with you later!"

The way he said all that to her was chilling because she knew what her husband was capable of. Especially when he appeared as calm as he was at that moment, fear rose to her chest. His eyes were cold and his jaw was tight.

"There's a car waiting for you outside, it will take you to the airport for your flight to the house in Spain."

"I have a lot of shit to clean up here thanks to you and your daughter. I can't afford to have liabilities during horombo."

Malantha obediently obliged, she wasn't allowed time to pack. She was told everything she needed would be provided so she found herself headed to East Midlands Airport.

Jack assembled his M21 sniper rifle in a small janitor's storage room on the top floor of Newarke Street multi-storey car park. Jack had done his due diligence so he knew there was not going to be any unwanted guests. The room had one little window overlooking the buildings below. There were several buildings surrounding the multi-storey car park which was the perfect cover. Like the other buildings around, it was also modern so it did not draw any attention.

Most importantly from his vantage point on the roof he could clearly watch Chris's penthouse. Even though the window he was looking out from was dirty, when he looked through his scope he could see The Wullcumb and the surrounding complex pretty good. Anyone lingering on the roof area of the penthouse was vulnerable to sniper shots. The large glass windows also gave Jack good visuals on the occupants. He got himself comfortably situated and waited, as patient as destiny looking at his phone awaiting further instruction from Reggie and Luke.

Luke was sitting in the truck and they were all communicating via text. Reggie texted as soon as he got buzzed into the complex and it wasn't long before he was in the elevator going up. His hands began to sweat and he thought his heart was going to pound out of his chest. Many scenarios had played out in his head of what could happen and in all of them, he hadn't imagined not making it alive except now. He suddenly thought what if they shot him as soon as he walked in.

The mere thought of walking to his death made him doubt himself. He also imagined a life without his mother and sister, how he wouldn't be able to live with himself if anything happened to them. Either way the odds were stacked against him, but if there was anything about Reggie Pereira, he was a fighter. So he buckled up and figured if anything was going to happen he wasn't going to take it lying down.

"Well well well! If it isn't Mr Prince Charming himself, welcome to my humble abode my friend," said Chris mockingly at Reggie who had been let in.

"Please Chris, let me see Carmen, is she ok?" He pleaded, making small steps towards where Chris was standing.

"Easy tiger. Stop right there and put your hands up."

Reggie calmly put his hands up and he immediately felt the guy who had opened the door behind him patting him down for weapons. As the man was frisking him, a shiver worked its way up his spine when he started to work his way below his waist.

"Come on Chris, you know I don't carry any weapons, just please let Carmen go man, you can take me."

Chris signalled the guy to stop because not only was Reggie outnumbered, but he was out muscled too, they all had guns.

"Relax, Reggie, come on let's have a drink," Chris said pointing to the bar with the gun to let Reggie know that he had no choice. There was a glass already poured for him, but he hesitated to drink thinking it may have been spiked.

"Come on Reggie. Drink up my friend. It's your favourite cognac, Louis XIII, the good stuff. I insist."

Reggie reluctantly took a sip of it and slowly swallowed before putting the glass down and looking around the room for Carmen. She wasn't in sight. It was just the three guys who were standing strategically around the room, two of them holding handguns, but he knew they probably all had weapons.

"Ok, I see we're not going to have as much fun as I intended with you Reggie. I knew you were going to be a fucking problem the moment you picked Carmen over Freya."

Chris signalled for the men to bring Carmen in and moments later they emerged from another door carrying a chair with Carmen tied up and duct tape wrapped over her mouth.

When Reggie saw Carmen he was overwhelmed with emotions. He had to fight back tears from rolling out his eyes. Without thought, he got up and yelled "Carmen" edging towards where she was.

Immediately Chris pointed his gun at Reggie and said, "Whoa! I told you she was okay didn't I? Be cool and sit back down." He was forcibly made to sit back on his stool and look at Carmen who couldn't say a word. Endless tears rolled down her moistened, unsettled face.

Seeing Reggie made a volcano of feelings erupt in her and she started trembling both from fear and relief because she hadn't seen him in a while. She thought of how life was unfair, for giving her the love of her life and then putting them both in these circumstances. The thought of them both dying and not fulfilling their promises to each other made everything worse.

Chris relished the surge of raw power. It was like being in the loins of a woman whom one had perused for a long time, subduing a superior enemy all at once and a thousand fold. The power consumed him and it was his time to shine and show Reggie that even guys who look like him could win. He ordered Reggie to move closer to where Carmen sat in the middle of the room and said, "now that we are all here, let's get this party started."

"I hated you from the first time I saw you Reggie, you represent everything I hate about guys like you."

"You think just because you look good the world owes you, well the world doesn't owe you shit."

He went over to Carmen and said, "She is beautiful isn't she?"

He extended his hand to her chin and tilted her face until their eyes met.

"I wanted Carmen for myself Reggie and maybe, just maybe I could have had her and her father would have had you for the sacrifice."

"But you are more slippery than we thought." Watching Carmen being handled like that cut up Reggie's insides and he pleaded for Chris to let her go once more.

Hearing Reggie's voice again made his blood boil and triggered him to go from anger to rage. Everybody in the room could sense the increased levels of unpredictability which had engulfed him.

"This has taken longer than it should have," he raised his pistol and aimed it at Carmen's head.

"This is your fault Reggie, you caused it, don't worry, you will see her soon, in hell."

"Chris! Please don't", Reggie cried out.

Carmen kicked and screamed, but to no avail as her screams was muffled by the duct tape covering her mouth. She glared at the gleaming gun-barrel that was pointed to her head. The helpless shrieks from Reggie made her realise she was not dreaming, this was real. It was a real 9.mm pistol staring at her right in the face. She looked into that deep, empty, ready to wish you good bye world hole. Reggie could not do anything to save her because one of the men had a gun aimed menacingly at him.

Click! Click! Chris cocked his gun and tightened his grip before squeezing the trigger. Carmen squeezed her eyes closed as hard as she could until they started to hurt. Every muscle and ligament in her body stiffened in anticipation of the bullet. Reggie was yelling "Chris No!" but he had made up his mind. He saw Chris's finger clenching the gun tighter. He knew he needed to do something about it, but there was a gun pointed at him too so he just froze. It was like a terrible nightmare, everything in slow motion.

At that moment, blood spattered all over Carmen's white top. Brain fragments dropped onto her breasts. The target's head split and in instant brains incinerated from the heat made her top look like a Dalmatian with red blood spots. With a sickening thud the lifeless body fell to the ground. The three men immediately hit the floor for cover and pointed their weapons in the direction where the fatal shot came from. A bullet had split Chris's head open. It cracked the glass and splintered the bar counter making a sound which they only heard after he'd been struck.

There was only one person in the room who knew where the bullet came from. Jack had fired the fatal shot from hundreds of yards away in the janitor's room at Newarke street multi-storey car park. When he moved closer to Carmen Chris had made him-self vulnerable to sniper fire by standing next to the glass doors. The rest were bewildered because they checked every nook and cranny of the penthouse for possible intruders. Knowing that Jack had actually executed as planned gave Reggie an adrenalin rush. He knew he had to seize the moment if they had any chance of making it out alive.

Reggie crawled behind the bar counter and drew the llama 82 which he had concealed in an ankle holster. Chris had sealed his fate by not allowing the man to frisk him properly. One of the men pointed to the bar to let the others know that Reggie was behind the counter. When Reggie propped himself up to be in a better position to see his enemies he made the glasses on the counter-shelving rattle. This clearly gave off his position.

A barrage of bullets flew towards him tearing and shuttering anything in their path. Although the bullets were punching holes on the bar counter they were not penetrating. Reggie dropped low to the ground to present a smaller target and waited till he had a clear shot of any of them. They was a short silence as one of the men tip toed from an angle toward the bar.

His senses were heightened, eyes bulging, scanning ready to shoot at anything that moved. He heard the man step on a piece of debris so he threw a wine glass in the opposite direction and the man shot in the same direction with panic. Reggie aimed at his leg and dropped him. He then rolled aside as his other leg swept out in an effort to get up and fired another two shots upwards into his abdomen and groin.

The gunplay was fairly loud so Reggie did not know whether Carmen was still alive or not, maybe one of the men had shot her dead. That thought alone fuelled his quest. A brass-jacketed slug flying like a drill bit snickered through the air punching a hole through flesh. It ripped a ragged wound channel through the muscles and internal organs of the second man.

He had once again appeared clear on Jack's scope so he let loose. The third guy who had his eye on Carmen witnessed bodies drop from his Boss to the latest victim so he was in utter confusion and panic. So much that he did not see that Carmen had managed to free her hands and reach for Chris's 9 mm which was next to his cold body. Without hesitation, she squeezed the trigger and blew his head off.

She was still holding the gun in total shock. The weight of the gun felt like an anchor to her tumultuous mind. Moments ago there had been a percussion of sounds from bullets, guns and screaming, now it was silent. The acrid smell from the cartridges lingered over the four motionless bodies scattered on the floor like wild vines. It was hard to ignore the smell of copious blood from them. Reggie was crouched in a corner holding his gun out in front of him ready to shoot at anything that moved. He had no idea how many bad guys there were so he did not want to be surprised. He was sweating profusely and some of it trickled in his eye making it itch, but didn't wipe it off or blink.

Carmen had dropped the gun to the floor and the horror of what had occurred finally hit her. She ripped off the duct tape from her mouth and broke out crying like a baby. Even though her hands were freed she was still tied to the chair. She felt so frail, drained with no energy to untie her-self. The silence seemed to confirm her worst fears. She imagined Reggie's body slumped cold behind the counter. Her crying soon faded to quiet mournful sobbing.

"If someone is going to kill me they will not find me waiting," he thought to himself.

He had picked up one of the men's revolvers for back up and cautiously edged ahead. Eyes peeled with both arms extended pointing his weapon in the direction of his footsteps. He stepped over the dead guy and emerged from the corner to see the other two guys also dead. Not seeing a woman's body on the floor sparked a tinker of hope which quickly grew into elation when he caught sight of Carmen. Her hair was over her face and it was enmeshed with blood, bone fragments and brain matter. Anyone else would not have been able to recognise her in that state. Not Reggie, he could pick her out from a crowd.

"Carmen, Carmen!", "Oh my God Reggie," he ran to embrace her, and untied the ropes which bound her. Overwhelmed with emotions it brought more tears, but a different kind of tears. No words were exchanged they hugged each other like they had never hugged any human being before. Reggie slid a Vacheron watch off one of the dead man's wrist and put it in his pocket.

They both had so many questions to ask each other, but it wasn't the right time to do so. They were literally in the middle of consecutive life sentences. Reggie informed Luke and Jack to come to the penthouse quickly via text. The fact that they were private investigators gave them extensive knowledge in CCTV equipment operation and in this case manipulation.

The mere location and private set-up of the penthouse meant that all the commotion did not raise any unwanted attention. If it did the neighbours would have dismissed it as one of Chris's parties which occasionally got loud. Luke and Jake had ways of getting rid of the bodies as well as the evidence so they immediately went to work while Carmen and Reggie made their way to his apartment.

They drove around in circles making sure no one was following them before driving straight to the apartment. They both looked for anything unusual indicating that someone had been there. Reggie was certain that nothing had been moved or touched since he was last there. He let her take a shower first and laid out his long sleeved t shirt and some socks on the bed so she could wear fresh clothes.

Carmen took a long shower in scalding hot water.

She somehow hoped that the hot water would wash away her sins and cleanse her. She was still trembling and every time she closed her eyes she saw alternating images of prior events. She washed her body with soap. The lather and water cascaded down her body. The weight of having killed another human being, all the killing that she was now a part of weighed her down to the floor. Palms against the shower floor she sobbed while rubbing and scrubbing herself. Her body had reached its breaking point and the only emotion she could work up to feeling was exhaustion. Carmen emerged from the steam-filled bathroom with a towel wrapped round her body and another wrapped round her head. Reggie went in and took his shower. He was in and out almost in a flash because he had so much to offload.

"I look ridiculous in these clothes," Carmen said raising both of her hands to show him how baggy they looked on her. She wanted to break the silence between them.

She also didn't want to seem weak and delicate at the same time.

"They look better on you than they do on me," he responded trying to ignore the fact that she looked attractive and beautiful in them. She was sitting on the edge of the bed stealing glimpses of him while she adjusted her outfit. His severe features held a charisma that awakened her sexually.

Abruptly she looked away, hating her quickened pulse, but Reggie already knew what he needed to do. He wanted to kiss her. From the look on her face he knew she wanted him to. He gently kissed her. The softness of her lips reminded him of the first time they locked lips. Carmen put her arms around him and kissed him back. Their bodies were yearning for each other in ways that super-seeded lust. Reggie ran his fingers through her hair exposing her ears.

The feeling was mesmerising when he grabbed her hips and pulled her closer to his powerful body. The warmth of her body, her silky soft skin and erotic posture made him want to make love to her right there and then. The sparkling ring on her finger reminded him of how much Carmen had changed him for the better. He had not been intimate with any other woman since meeting her.

It dawned on him that he had to be truthful with her about his relationship with Malantha. Ever since he found out that Malantha was Carmen's mother, he had been both resentful and angry. Mostly angry with him-self for being so careless. He would get angry with Malantha and Carmen because he battled with the possibility of their relationship being a fraud.

Was the basis of their relationship based on luring him for the sacrifice? Was Carmen in it from the beginning? All these questions had accumulated in his head for so long he had to get some answers. Looking at the ring on her finger made him realise how bad he really wanted to start a family with her. Maybe they never truly would. He didn't know how things would be after telling her what he was about to tell her. There was a very strong possibility of losing her. The thought made his heart ache like it never had before. Needless to say Reggie brushed aside his fears and pulled back from her. She followed him because her body was ready in every single way. She wanted him.

She focused her gaze on him. Uncontrollable tremors of desire rippling through her and said, "I miss you so much Reggie, I want you so bad."

She breathed heavily. She was ready. He cleared his throat.

"Carmen, there's something I have to tell you."

Judging by his demeanour she quickly sobered up from the sexual drunkenness she had been under the influence of. She looked at him in askance "okay." She figured that the fact that he had brought this up at this moment meant that it was important.

Knowing that what he had to say would be devastating he pulled back even more and talked in a sombre tone, "there's no easy way to say this." "No easy way, easy way to say what?" Her eyes swept at Reggie's face searching for signs of reason.

"I knew your mother before I met you Carmen."

"Before I met you, my life was a lot different, I was a different man."

"I am not proud of who I was."

"I used to party a lot and entertain a lot of women."

Before he could carry on Carmen passionately interrupted, "Reggie I don't care about your past", he interjected in the same sombre tone as before.

"Please let me finish because this has been weighing heavily on me since I found out Malantha is your mother." "Like I said, way before I met you, I met your mother and."

"And what Reggie?" there was a slight pause before he responded.

"We kind of had a relationship, well not a real relationship, but a physical one, I'm sorry Carmen."

She could not believe the words coming out of his mouth. This was the man she loved and he was saying things she'd only ever seen and heard in movies.

"Wait a minute Reggie; you said you had a physical relationship with my mom?"

"You had sex with my mom?" "Is that what you are telling me right now?"

"Answer me!" She snarled at him punching his chest.

"Answer me Reggie, did you sleep with my mom, Oh my God!"

Her voice quavered and she buried her head into her hands. She cried uncontrollably, the type of crying that comes in horrible, diaphragm hurting spasms. He tried to hold her, but she pushed him off and twisted away. She ran off into the bathroom crying and locked herself in.

It almost felt like someone had taken a knife and stabbed her in the heart, then twisted it forty-five degrees for good measure. Carmen felt like the world's biggest fool. The man who she had been so in love with and was willing to die for had turned out to be nothing, but a liar and a cheat. Not only that, but he had slept with her own mother. Waves on nausea washed over her and she vomited into the toilet before sitting on the lid crying her eyes out. In a rather sadistic way it felt worse than the feeling she got from having to take a man's life.

This hurting was different. The anguish made her wish death for her mother who had given birth to her. She had been a source of great misery. She didn't want anything to do with anyone or anything, everything seemed pointless.

Reggie stood by the door with his shoulders slumped. The debauchery that once garnered him considerable respect amongst his peers had now left his relationship in tatters. Complete and utter hollowness filled him from crown to crouch. Hearing her sob like that made him feel less of a man. He was still haunted by the trauma of seeing his father being abusive towards his mother. It had made him swear to never harm a female, yet there he was. There was nothing he could do to help her because he was the source of her pain. The door which separated them seemed to represent a new genesis. To him it felt like the closeness they once shared was now no more. His own mental chastisement had ignited a bonfire of guilt since he found out. The guilt had made him lose a few pounds so as tough as this may have been, in a way he was relieved. Reggie felt as if he had taken a mental broom and resolutely swept away the cobwebs and dust that had accumulated in his mind.

Carmen cried and cried until she had nothing left, then cried some more. In the end it subsided to gentle sobbing then complete silence. The only sounds apparent were the hissing and buzzing of electrical gadgets mixed in with the ethereal music of the trees outside. Reggie sat on the floor leaning against the bathroom door. His head faced the ceiling and his eyes were closed.

Easily an hour elapsed, in that moment time had no relevance. He would have sat there forever waiting for a signal from her to fully explain him-self. A signal surely did come. It was one he'd expected and dreaded. He watched the four claw solitaire 18 karat white gold ring sliding out from underneath the door. Reggie's heart sank into his stomach as an intense feeling of trepidation pierced through him.

He said the only thing he could think of, and it came from the bottom of his soul, "Carmen, I am sorry."

"I am going to tell you everything. Everything, exactly how it happened. Then if you want to leave me you can. If you want to go right now I won't stop you, but I am going to tell you everything and you can make your final decision," he pleaded.

Reggie pulled himself together, wiped his face, clasped his hands and started to explain how he met Malantha. He revealed how he met her at a store while shopping for a suit. He also owned up to the secret rendezvous at the mansion in Tilton on the hill. He emphasised that it happened before they met. He only found out when they came to visit her in Wales. Reggie explained to Carmen that it was the main reason he'd been distant after the accident. He felt guilty and ashamed.

He explained how a cloud of confusion bestowed him when he found out that his girlfriend's parents wanted to kill him. He automatically thought that she was part of Cilocy. Carmen had been quietly listening until that point. She unlocked the door and walked past Reggie avoiding eye contact. She sat back on the bed.

Reggie continued, "I mean you all wear the same watches, so when I started putting the pieces of the puzzle together, I started to doubt you Carmen. I thought you were part of this whole secret society."

"I have never been involved in any of whatever it is my mother and father are involved with. Do you think I would have gone to Chris's looking for you if I was?" Carmen told Reggie that she knew her parents had dealings with some kind of secret society. She said she had no idea about the magnitude of it all until she stumbled upon the weird room in the cellar at their new house. She told Reggie that she found photos of his family in his father's study. She knew they had killed Freya like Chris confirmed. The revelations brought about some clarity and made them both realise they had been used as pawns for Cilocy.

Reggie told her detailed information about the organisation as described to him by Aleixo. It gave her a vivid peek into the evil world of her parents. At this point Reggie was not even thinking about redemption. The conversation exacerbated the rage and anger he had for Mr Dean. He pleaded with her to assist him in rescuing his mother and sister. After he had rescued her from Chris and crew she thought it was only right to return the favour. Carmen knew she wasn't going to let Reggie off the hook for sleeping with her mother. Her anger was too fresh with betrayal to exonerate him. She tried to sort through her sentiments to rationalise them. Mixed emotions washed over her, swallowing her like a ship at sea.

CHAPTER 17
Penance

The taxi roared down the A50 and Malantha sat in the back morosely contemplating. She was definitely not ready to go and stay in Spain. Her husband had not specified the length of stay. She assumed it was going to be until things calmed down or at least until they were done with horombo. Either way she had no say. She had been perfectly programmed by Rodney Dean to do as he wanted her to do without any questions asked.

Her life had been so fast paced. At times, she wondered if it really was the life she wanted to live. Malantha came from a family of educators. She was destined to be a great teacher because it ran in the family. She drew a lot of strength from her father who left just before she started high school. She still didn't know why he left, but she suspected that it was something to do with her mother wanting another baby.

On numerous occasions, she overheard their heated arguments over her mother's infidelities caused by the fact. She often recalled feeling guilt for being the only child. When her father left Malantha felt fear, abandoned, guilt, hurt, worry and sadness. Her world turned upside down. The day he left, a cold winter morning. He woke her up from her sleep, kissed her on the forehead and hugged her. That morning he held on to her a little tighter than usual.

Her little ears could feel his heart beating fast. She knew something was not right. When the door slammed shut and her father walked out that day, she knew she would never see him again. That was the last day she ever saw him. She felt as if it was her fault he left, like she had done something wrong. Her father died years later in a senior citizen home in Manchester where he had relocated to.

Her whole life, since early childhood she had been daddy's little girl. Even at her grown age she still remembered her father's constant praise. "You will make me proud one day Mala, just like I did for my papa" he used to tell her. She was an only child and he used to tell her that the greatest honour bestowed upon a man was for him to have a daughter, and for the daughter to follow his footsteps.

For that reason, she had worked hard to become a professor of linguistics at De Montfort University. She was fluent in many languages and that's how she met a young impressionable businessman who spoke Portuguese. Men usually fought for her attention because she was stunning, fearless, outgoing with a personality to match. Malantha was self-aware from an early age. She knew she was attractive so the ability to attract men was not an issue. She was very clear on how she wanted her life to be and she did not have a problem telling anyone about it.

The budding businessman was not particularly good looking. She liked his skin which was the colour of deep chocolate. When he introduced himself at an event he'd sponsored at the University she liked his smile. From that day they kept in contact and soon started meeting up regularly. It soon became apparent that they both had a mutual appreciation for the finer things in life. She liked that Rodney was a take charge kind of guy. He seemed to have a solution to every problem. From picking the restaurant they would go to eat, to actually helping her get ahead in her career. The relationship soon blossomed into a romance.

Rodney was the king of grand gestures. He definitely made her feel special and they did everything together from taking trips and handling finances. He was organised in ways that reminded her of how her father was. It didn't take long before they got married and had their daughter Carmen. What started off as being organised soon turned into obsession and control. She started noticing that he didn't like her around people he didn't know and that's around the same time she found out that he was the leader of a secret society.

This seemed to occupy the majority of his time. She started to miss the attention she used to get from him. He was a feared leader who was violent and there were fatal consequences for crossing him. He openly spoke about some of the things he had done to people. This was his way of keeping her in line.

There were times she wanted to end the relationship and just leave, but in a way she enjoyed the fruits of being Mrs Dean. She found her own ways of coping. She would sometimes self-medicate with alcohol. Deep down she knew she probably needed to seek some professional help, some counselling or something. She would have had to be secretive about that because Rodney wouldn't approve. The young male students at the University gave her a lot of attention.

She looked much younger than her age. So she would have discreet intimate relationships with some of them. This was easy to do because Rodney was always somewhere doing God knows what. It became normal for her and she even started having affairs with men she met either online or randomly which was how she met Reggie. She regretted bringing him to the house. It was the reason she was in the car headed to the airport.

She regretted not protecting her daughter and not allowing her to live the life she wanted. She regretted not spending enough time to get to know her. There were a lot of things she regretted, but the biggest one was being Mrs Dean. She longed for a normal life.

Often while in public places she would watch with envy other couples holding hands. She noticed the little public displays of affection and longed for that type of closeness. As time went on

Malantha realised something. She had spread herself like a flower in the sunshine, and now, like that flower when the night fell, and the damp chill crept on, she folded her own sorrow within her own breast. The relationship she had with her husband had been nothing, but a straw house built on sand, incapable of weathering life's storms.

Over the course of time, nothing made sense to her anymore. All the structures that had supported her throughout her life, the foundation upon which her paradigms had been built had collapsed. All that was left was material things which really didn't mean anything to her anymore. She didn't want to be a prisoner to material gains while sacrificing her inner happiness. She longed for a good marriage, a marriage of strong character and united strength, a partnership not a dictatorship.

As the self- reflection took place she hadn't noticed the tears sliding down her cheeks until the driver asked if she was alright. She wiped the tears from her eyes, being careful not to smudge her make-up. Never before had she ever felt so strongly about breaking free from the chains that bound her. The way the taxi driver was in full control of the vehicle gave her a new revelation. It was the perfect metaphor for what she needed to do, and that was to take control of her life. She needed to make new drastic changes starting with realising that the most important thing in her life was her daughter.

"Change of plans, turn around and take me back to Leicester please", she ordered. Instead of taking the first exit to merge onto the M1 for East Midlands Airport, the driver took the fourth exit back to Leicester. She made a decision that would change her life forever. Terrifying as it was that she had gone against Rodney's instructions, it felt liberating.

She checked herself into a low-key three star hotel knowing that it would be an unlikely location for her husband to find her. Malantha was not about to under estimate how resourceful her husband was. She had written all the important numbers on a piece of paper and tossed her phone in case it was being tracked. She also generously tipped the taxi driver and told him to say he had dropped her off at the airport if anyone asked.

What would she even say to her daughter if she was to speak to her? Would she even entertain the idea of talking? What would stop her from putting the phone down and not ever wanting to have anything to do with her? In all fairness that wouldn't be an over-reaction based on the amount of scars she'd inflicted on Carmen's life. Without a doubt, Malantha was undeserving of a mother of the year award, but she owed it to her daughter to come clean. To at least try and make amends. It may have been too late, but never the less she needed to get a hold of her before her husband did.

She sat on the frayed yellow corduroy armchair next to the square mahogany table where she had placed the paper with phone numbers. Malantha took a deep breath before she started punching the numbers into the burner phone she'd got. Waiting for Carmen to pick up was like waiting for a judge to pass sentence after a guilty verdict. Every minute, every ring brought about a mixed bag of feelings. She was speculative, terrified, nervous and contemplative all at the same time.

"Hello, hello who is this?" Carmen had hesitated to pick up the call because it wasn't a number she recognised. She was about to terminate the call when she heard a familiar voice pleading.

"I'm so sorry Carmen, please forgive me. Please sweet heart forgive me for everything I've ever done, I am so ashamed."

It was her mother on the other line, sobbing and asking to be heard. Hearing her mother's voice awakened the anguish she felt towards her. The painful memories of how her parents had always ruined her relationships came flooding back in full force.

"How dare you, how dare you mom", angrily talking into the phone. The anger in her tone matched her facial expressions. Even though she was not in front of her Malantha could feel that she'd hurt her in ways that were probably impossible to repair. She desperately wanted to make her feel better. So she attentively listened while her daughter spilled her heart out.

"What kind of evil mother are you, to get your own flesh and blood killed, your own flesh and blood. How sick is that huh? Is this what this call is about huh! To check if I'm alive or dead, is that what this is mom? Answer me!" she screamed into the phone which gave off an uncomfortable feedback on the other end.

"Am I even your real daughter? I mean, you and dad have really gone to extreme lengths to destroy my life. What did I do to deserve this? All I wanted was a normal childhood, but you robbed me of that. You have chased away every single one of my boyfriends and now I come to find out that my mom slept with my man. How do you think I feel right now mom, huh, how do you think I feel."

She went on to tell Malantha about what she found in her dad's study. She told her that she knew they wanted to kill Reggie like they did Freya.

"Sweetheart I know I'm a terrible mother, I have no excuses to give you, but believe me when I tell you. I would never knowingly let any harm come unto you. There are a lot of things I haven't been honest about in the past. I want to make it right. You have every right to be angry with me Carmen,, but right now your life and mine are in danger. I am calling from a different number because I destroyed my old phone. Carmen your father is a very dangerous man, I know you now realise that. You say someone tried to kill you. I have no doubt that your father sent them to retrieve the documents you took. Please be very careful. I'm supposed to be in Spain right now, but I don't feel safe."

Carmen and Reggie suspected that the Mr Dean and Malantha were the ones holding his parents hostage. When Carmen confronted her mother about it she vehemently denied having any knowledge of it.

"Again it's all your father's doing" she added.

"I can guarantee that he will not stop till he gets his own way. I know you are mad at me, but we are running out of time. Please allow me this one chance to make it up to you and Reggie, please. The least I can do is save yours and Reggie's life. I may never right all my wrongs, but let me try."

Based on everything Carmen had zero trust for her mother. Yet for the first time she could sense her being sincerely apologetic and remorseful.

"You are everything I never was Carmen, determined and ready to give up the universe for the things you believe in. You have turned out to be the woman I never was. You did it all on your own. Just like your name says, you are a garden, you deserve to flourish."

Carmen didn't want to start processing or gauging the levels of her mother's sincerity, but she knew they had to be allies if they were to save Reggie's family. Her mother was the perfect ally to have because she knew her father the best. They agreed to drive to the hotel she was staying so they could put together a plan. When the call finished Reggie was already preparing and checking his ammo. Carmen was still saturated in a pool of emotions when suddenly there was a knock on the door.

The collective mind immediately started to worry. Reggie pulled the Llama 82 from his backpack and tucked it into his waistband at the small of his back and pulled his shirt over it. He stepped into the hallway and slowly advanced towards the front door. He intercepted Carmen who was making her way to him and put his finger over his mouth as a sign to keep quiet.

Reggie pointed to the bedroom for Carmen to go and she retreated without any objections. Whoever was at the door must have felt like the occupants where not moving to the door fast enough because they began pounding the door in a way that startled Reggie and Carmen.

The thought of having been tracked down and cornered by Mr Dean's people sent a strong pulse of nervousness through his body. He had already survived another gun battle with the help of Jack and Luke. If anything was going to go down he was on his own. His gun was fully loaded and drawn. He was more than willing to engage. His body started to tense up as he looked through the peephole.

There were two men dressed in what he made out to be cheap suits. It was weird because the pedigree of Mr Dean's people wore very high quality suits like the one's he preferred. They looked fairly relaxed so he immediately eliminated the possibility of them being a threat. He put his gun away before pulling the door ajar slightly.

"How can I help you gentlemen?" he asked sounding as genuine as he could.

The heavily built guy in front answered, confidently, "My name is Officer Richardson and this in my partner officer Timms. We are with the Leicester Constabulary. We are looking for a Mr Reggie Pereira."

"Can I ask what this is about?" Reggie asked.

"Are you Mr Reggie Pereira sir?" Reggie responded by saying he was.

"Your name popped up during an investigation about a recent Incident at London St Pancreas station. You are a potential witness to the case which is still under investigation so we just wanted to take an official statement that's all."

"Do you want the statement now? I was in the middle of something at the moment." "That's fine; we will give you a couple of days to come to the police station. Here take my card; all my contacts are there if you have any questions. See you soon."

Reggie politely took the card. He was acting as normal as he could and he gave off a cooperative aura. When he was sure they were gone he locked the door and went into the bedroom where Carmen was.

"Fuck! This is the last thing I need," he yelled slamming the card on the dresser.

"What do they want?" Carmen asked after looking at the card and realising it was the police.

"They want a statement from me about that situation I told you with Aleixo fuck!"

"Well if it happened like you said it did, then we shouldn't worry about anything, right?"

There was a slight twinkle in Reggie's eye when he realised she had just said, "We" instead of "you."

It meant that she still imagined them being together, even if it was at a subconscious level. Either way it made him smile inwardly. He explained to Carmen that having the police sniffing around their movements and whereabouts would further complicate things. If they dug up enough dirt, they would end up connecting them with Chris's situation and who knows what else. After all, it was no secret that Mr Dean had some of the police in his pocket.

Syston Guest House located on Fosse road was the perfect hideout for Malantha. It was an old Victorian house converted into a hotel. It was very low key that one wouldn't have imagined it to be a hotel based on the building's exterior character. The hardwood floors made a loud creaking noise that echoed throughout the hallways. Normally it would have been an annoyance, but like an alarm system it helped Malantha hear if someone was walking up towards her room. She rose from the chair soon as she heard the boards creaking. She unlocked the door and immediately embraced her daughter in a tight hug. Carmen resisted the urge not to return the gesture, but she couldn't bring herself not comfort her mother who broke down crying.

There was a moment or awkward silence when all three of them were finally in the same room. To deflect and diffuse the awkwardness Reggie spoke, "so how do we rescue my mother and sister? Do you have an idea where they are?" He avoided making eye contact with Malantha and stared off into nothingness, contemplating if he would ever get used to seeing her as his mother in law.

"Tomorrow is Friday; all the kumoz will be at the house for horombo. We cannot wait for them to find us. If we are to have any fighting chance at all, we need to utilise the element of surprise. We have to take the fight to them. It will be the last thing they expect. It will also give us some clues of where your mother and sister are," Malantha said in a more authoritative manner than before.

CHAPTER 18
7 Hotoft Road

"Do you remember the body they pulled out from the river Soar the other week? The body we couldn't identify? Well the dental records are back." Officer Richardson was fixing himself a cup of strong coffee. Strong caffeine in the morning was a religious routine. He poured another cup for officer Timms and they both walked out the small kitchen to their desks which were opposite each other.

The body's dental records lay on the desk next to the computer. Richardson handed over the file to Timms who was half sitting on the edge of the desk. He put his coffee down, opened the file and focused his attention on the yellow form with the ante-mortem dental records. "Our victim's name is Joao Silva, not your typical name around here" Timms said while flipping through the paperwork. He pulled out a pink sheet which had the postmortem information and his eyes swept continuously across the page as he read it.

Autopsy results revealed that the victim had suffered strangulation injuries probably caused by having a ligature around his throat. His body was then dumped in the river in the hopes that it wouldn't be found. It was spotted by an old couple walking their dog one morning and they called the police. "You know what's funny? In the last couple of weeks there have been a lot of incidents and a couple of homicides involving victims with Spanish names.

Do you think it's a coincidence or I'm over thinking?" Officer Timms asked, placing the file back on the desk.

"Firstly those names are Portuguese origin not Spanish and secondly, you actually have a point," Richardson responded.

He asked his colleague to focus his attention onto the computer screen so he could show him something.

He pointed to the missing person's report which had been filed by the victim's family. It gave the victim's details as Joao Silva of number 7 Hotoft Road, Humber stone.

The victim was described as being six feet tall weighing just over two hundred pounds. They immediately knew that it would have taken more than one person to subdue him. His hair was described as being black, brown eyes and fair skin. The information on the missing person's report matched their victim.

They made the unpleasant drive to his residence to notify the family that his body had been found. Upon further investigation, they soon found out that Joao was actually Reggie's uncle. This certainly raised their eyebrows and made them want to dig further so they could connect the dots.

Kainga struggled to maintain both her calm and her footing as the kumoz led them through a maze of unannounced obstacles, including stairs and several doorways. Esther was right behind her.

The whole ordeal was terrifying to them because they had no clue why they were taken. They hadn't been starved or tortured, but since their arrival at the place the atmosphere had been so filled with evil they could barely draw breath.

Esther and her mother were kid knapped, blindfolded and taken to an unknown location. There were kept separate so neither one knew what was happening to the other. When the blindfolds were finally removed they were sitting on a wooden alter. The altar had engravings of weird creatures and other demonic insignia. Hands and feet were bound by chains which were pegged onto the floor. Candles provided all the lighting in the room. The altar was the best lit area in the room because there were two free standing candelabras, one on each side.

It was time to do the horombo sacrifice and all the kumoz were gathered and ready to start the ceremony. Esther and her mom knew they were in the realm of dark energy which was distressing and perplexing. There was an unsettling quietness, it made them realise they was nothing they could have said to the make the kumoz placated. Their hooded cloaks only exposed the kumoz eyes and necks so it was impossible to recognise any of them.

One of them walked close past Esther to go and do something on the shrine. Perhaps light a candle or something. The shrine was about ten feet away from them. She noticed the kumoz holding a staff made of what seemed to be human bones. All of them were holding these staffs. It sent her into a frenzy of anxiety and fear. She felt her scalp crawling at the thought of how the sticks were possibly made.

Kainga's blood pressure dramatically shot up. They were leaning against each other's backs and Esther could feel her mother struggling to breathe. She started whispering bible verses in an attempt to calm her mother down. They were petrified and trembling so much it caused the chains to rattle making echoey eerie sound effects.

The Kumoz licked their fingers and ran them on each other's neck in customary greeting and showing allegiance. "Blessed are the destroyers of fear and chance, cursed are those who think god will intervene for they shall be shorn the power of Gorah" they chanted. To Esther and kainga the words alone conveyed no fear, but the implication that something was seeking admission did.

Mr Dean was wearing his cloak and ready to emerge from a secret doorway straight to the basement were the ceremony was about to take place. Horombo was very important in Cilocy because the blood was a potent source of nourishment for the deity. The sacrifice of human life was the ultimate offering to the Gorah. It was the first time they had not been able to get the actual male sacrifice required so it made him a bit uneasy.

To make up for that they were going to offer the deity two sacrifices. One with the bloodline required which was Esther, the daughter of a former Cilocy member. Kainga's blood would be a way of showing gratitude. He had lost all trust in Chris who had failed to deliver, and when he tried to contact him he didn't pick up. Rodney Dean had been born with the gift that enabled the deity to speak through him. Being in the presents of the Kumoz chanting made the possession faster and he had a special potion he drank to summon the spirits.

Mr Dean adjusted his outfit before taking a swig out of a glass vial which contained the potion. He strapped a red cross to his neck. The syrupy mixture left his raw throat burning. He pushed the door open and slowly started walking towards the shrine. The crowd parted like the red sea, giving him a clear path to walk to the altar. As the chanting got louder his eyes, soul and spirit started to transform. The voices rattle snaked in his head.

"Simukah Gorah, Simukah Gorah, Simukah Gorah," he commanded in a menacing voice much different to his own. The veins on his body especially the ones on his neck started to spasm rapidly. Like some form intravenous fluids were violently entering the body. The gauntly appearance he already had was now very pronounced. When he reached the altar all the Kumoz where kneeling, except four who were surrounding the altar. One of them unchained Esther, yanked her off the pedestal and chained her back close to the base of the altar. She screamed for help on top of her lungs, but not a soul paid attention. In-fact no one even looked her way. It was as if everything was rehearsed to perfection. It was just all movement and chanting without direct conversation.

Kainga pinched her eyes closed as tightly as possible, wishing she could make the terrible thing that was walking towards her go away. She prayed and wished she could levitate away. She felt her legs being fastened by some metal ornaments which felt cold on her skin. Her hands were clamped down in a crucifix position. Tears were flowing out from her eyes the whole time while she prayed. She had no energy left to put up a fight.

She just let them have their way. Even when they ripped her top off exposing her chest she barely resisted. It was Esther who screamed and pleaded with them to stop. She was positioned in a way that she couldn't see what was happening. She could only imagine.

The kumoz picked up a dagger from the illuminated ghoulish shrine and handed it to the Gorah reincarnate. Blood was running from his eyes and mouth. He growled some esoteric words while he slowly pulled the dagger from its scabbard. The large room broke out into sinister jeers edging the Gorah to accept the offering. He slowly raised his hands high in the air and waited, making sure of his target.

Kainga opened her eyes and caught sight of the gleaming blade. She cried out and instinctively tried to use her hands to defend herself. The effort was useless because her hands were secured. Mr Dean who was now fully possessed by the Gorah plunged the knife into the side of Kainga's neck. He severed the artery and then raked the keenly honed edge through her larynx and her jugular.

Blood spurt out like air escaping from a tyre. She shrieked, made a sound as thin and sharp as a sliver of ice. He pulled the blade free, raised his hands again and brought down heavily on her chest. The knife penetrated all the way to the hilt.

Arteries were ruptured and blood was everywhere. The chanting had intensified and Kainga was dead. Some of her mother's blood had spattered on her hair and face. Esther screamed all she could until her voice was gone. She wept helplessly bound next to the altar. Her whole body shivered, clothed in the remnants of what had been once a well put together high street outfit. Her sobs were drowned by the jeers of the jubilant Kumoz. Mr Dean's growls trailed away as he bent over the body aggressively pulling open the recent chest wound.

Cracking ribs out of the way he slowly removed Kainga's heart. He lifted the red flesh to his nose, sniffed it briefly before tearing out a huge chunk with his already bloody teeth. It was very apparent that Mr Dean was harbouring a demonic entity with an insatiable appetite for blood. The four Kumoz collected blood from the body and walked around smearing it on others. They all lined up in order and dipped their hands in a bronze grail by the shrine containing blood. They smeared the blood on the deity's face as they walked past chanting "Simukah Gorah, Simukah Gorah." The ceremony was in full swing. It was now time to give the Gorah the ultimate sacrifice. What was left of Kainga's body was removed from the altar for dismemberment. They replaced her with her daughter's body which was young, fresh and of the desired bloodline.

Reggie had worn the Vacheron Constatin watch he took from one of the guys he killed at Chris's apartment. This made it easier for him to gain entrance into the mansion because that was pretty much the way everyone recognised each other. Malantha and Carmen wore their watches too, and all three of them were in the same attire as the rest of the kumoz. Even though both Malantha and Carmen knew their way around the house, on this day it would have been difficult to gain access into the basement. The easiest way would have been to use the cellar access, but it would have drawn the wrong attention. The only choice they had was to use the entrance everyone used.

They blended in well with the Kumoz and they did what everyone was doing trying their best not to stand out. For Reggie it was hard for him to hold back the urge of wanting to walk up to the front. The low lighting did not allow him to clearly identify the identities of the two silhouetted figures on the altar. They were right at the back so they had to blend in and follow the sequence until they reached the front.

The jeering and chanting made it difficult to ascertain the order of events. To Reggie and Carmen the ceremony seemed rather mediocre. In the midst of the chaos they had missed the first sacrifice. When they got closer to the front Reggie clearly recognised her sister who was in the process of being chained to the altar for the last part of the sacrifice.

Unlike her mother Esther resisted with all her might. The Kumoz struggled to chain her down to the bloody altar and she tried her best to delay the inevitable. She wasn't going to go down without a fight. She noticed that more Kumoz where making their way to the altar to assist. The other two held her legs together to stop her from kicking.

They clipped the metal rings in place while the others held her hands. She realised that everything that was going on must have been an allegory of the event. The Gorah was already in position with dagger in hand. Suddenly one of the Kumoz pulled out a gun and put it under the chin of another and squeezed the trigger. His head snapped back and hit the ground dead. The coppery smell of blood and fired cordite filled the air.

Within seconds there was complete mayhem. The familiar cracking sounds of a gun going off made everyone panic. Like a trained killing robot the Kumoz pointed his gun at anyone who was close to the altar and squeezed knocking them down like dominos. Carmen and Malantha ultimately made their way to the altar. They were armed with handguns as well and shot at anything or anyone who got in the way. When Mr Dean unknowingly moved a little closer to Esther she sunk her teeth into his leg through the gown. Mr Dean who was still possessed by the Gorah let out a loud growl of pain as he tried to wretch his leg loose. Carmen shrieked as she bit deeper into his thigh tearing out the fabric like a German Shepard biting a stuffed dummy. She tore off flesh and blood spurted fourth from it.

He staggered desperately trying to get her off him. The dagger had slipped out of his arms and fell to the ground. Esther's eyes were now huge black pools that glittered with animalism. She made guttural sounds from deep inside her throat and came off with a big chunk of flesh which she spat out. Her mouth was open, blood and spittle drooling from it. Still growling with pain Mr Dean stood half off balanced flailing his arms in the air, moving his fingers like claws of a gigantic ocean crab.

Reggie walked over to where Mr Dean was slumped over and pointed the gun in between his eyes. "Vejo você no inferno" (see you in hell)," he *mutted* before pulling the trigger. He fell to the ground completely lifeless. Reggie stood over him and shot him twice again in the chest to make sure.

He unchained his sister and they affectionately embraced. He handed her the dagger for protection and they started to head out of the mansion. He used one of the candles to set fire to the shrine. Reggie had instructed Carmen and Malantha to puncture the exposed gas pipes in the cellar. Malantha poured some kerosene she found all over the rooms she could access easily. There was a lot of smoke and confusion. A chaotic rush to get out and some Kumoz had taken off their gowns. Some people were trampled over in the stampede as everything seemed to catch on fire to the point where there was zero visibility.

By the time all four of them got to the front door almost the entire ground floor was ablaze. Flames blasted out from the windows and the people still inside screamed. You could see blackened hands moving in the flames until they were no more. The smoke thickened the air like a fire tyre in a country lot. Outside the mansion there were people who were rolling on the grass trying to put out the flames on their bodies. Some were screaming in pain with their skin peeled off or burnt to unrecognisable zombie like states.

The scent of the charred bodies was nauseating and putrid. It smelt like leather being tanned over a flame. Everyone's concern was safety and rescue. Seemingly oblivious to it all Reggie, Malantha, Carmen and Esther blended into the groups that were now forming outside. It was inevitable that the fire service was on its way. They managed to inconspicuously vacate the premises and drive off before any emergency services crew or police arrived.

CHAPTER 19
Coalville

"We believe that someone tampered with the surveillance, notice how the camera jumps from this shot where the delivery guy approaches to where he is driving off" said the gentleman from the video surveillance department. The footage was from The Wullcumb in the city centre where a multiple homicide had occurred. Well known playboy Chris De Mayo who lived the ultimate bachelor lifestyle had been murdered in his penthouse along with some of his associates.

"Word around town is the guy was Leicester's version of Hugh Hefner. He might have been caught with his hands in the cookie jar. Whoever did this to him must have been very pissed. It was definitely a professional hit" officer Timms said, handing over pictures of the evidence collected at the scene to Richardson.

"Multiple shell casings and also looks like they was a sniper involved judging by this," Richardson added pointing at a gory photo of Chris's head blown up and another photo of a boat tailed hollow point from a sniper rifle.

He swivelled back and forth in his chair, in a half-circle motion scratching his head as if he was calculating a simple math problem. Timms grimaced as he spun "can you stop spinning? I'm struggling to think." "Sorry mate." He stopped and concentrated on what Timms was saying.

Richardson put his elbows on the table and rested his chin in his hands as he listened with rapt attention.

"So when I got Chris's phone records back, you won't believe what I unearthed. I saw a number that was familiar and when I looked at our other cases guess what? It was Reggie Pereira's number."

"You're kidding me mate "Richardson shouted leaning back in his chair and folding his fingers together, he looked up towards the ceiling's corner and thought about where to start.

"I have a funny feeling about this Reggie character, something tells me he knows a lot about some of these mysterious cases of late. Which reminds me, he still hasn't showed up to give us his statement. Let me give him a call and ask him to come to the station as soon as."

Officer Richardson looked for his number on file and picked up the phone on his desk to dial. He tilted his head to one side and put the phone to his ear. It rang continuously before going to voicemail. "Time to do some gold old fashioned police work" Richardson said trying not to over emphasise his frustration. They both grabbed their jackets and headed out.

The two detectives pulled up at Reggie's apartment. Richardson knocked on the door several times, but no one answered. Timms tried to peep through the window to see if anyone was in. Even though the blinds were slightly open the lace curtains made it impossible to see anything. After several attempts they went back to the car and decided to drive over to Joao's house since he was Reggie's uncle.

They were unsure about the relationship Reggie had with his uncle's family so expectations were low as far as getting any leads. Timms came up with a strategy which they thought could yield results. He figured they would happily assist if they gave them the impression that Reggie was in possible danger from the same people who killed Joao.

Joao's family said they did not really know much about Reggie's life and in recent times they hardly saw him. The only information they got was an address for Reggie's mother. When they drove all the way to Coalville where Reggie's mother lived there was no one at the residence. A neighbour told them that they hadn't seen anyone come in or out of the premises in a while.

She also told them that a car there'd never seen before had come and taken Esther and her mother under bizarre circumstances. The fast thinking neighbour had written the registration number down in case anything happened. Richardson wrote the registration down and they headed back to the station with little or no information at all to work with.

When they arrived back at the station the chief inspector was waiting for them. Apparently there had been new developments on the case. Richardson and Timms were instructed by their superior to hand over evidence files for the case to him so he could pass it on to Scotland Yard who were going to pick up the case. That came as a shock to the two officers who knew they were in complete control of the case and hadn't missed any deadlines. They tried to convince him otherwise, but he was unwavering. He emphasised that they had to surrender every bit of information they had about that case and concentrate on other cases.

As this was a direct order they ended up obeying the request even though it seemed unorthodox. Richardson held on to the notes with the registration number of the alleged vehicle which had picked up Esther and Kainga. He rang his old buddy who worked as a traffic officer in the neighbouring city of Derby. He asked him to run the plates through the system and they came back as being registered to a local plumbing company. Richardson searched the internet to see who owned the company and to his disbelief it was co-owned by a Mr Rodney Dean and Mr Warren Casey. Warren Casey was his chief inspector. Richardson had potentially opened up a big can of worms.

CHAPTER 20
Blood Thirst

It had been 10 months after they left England in a hurry for a totally different environment in America. Reggie had worked in real estate for a long time, so through his connections he managed to arrange a safe haven for them away from their past life. They all moved into a comfortable home in the leafy suburbs of Decatur located approximately 5 miles northeast of downtown Atlanta.

Reggie had managed to get himself a job working for a small local real estate company. Malantha opened a little flower shop on Sycamore Drive which introduced her to the upper echelon of the city. Needless to say they had all lost loved ones so even though the new life was a breath of fresh air, everyone tended to get their moments. Esther especially had it the worst. She suffered from melancholia brought on by the gruesome killing of her mother. For the most part she stayed at home and did not really try to get familiar with her new surroundings. Carmen set up an online clothing company which she ran from home. Since finding out that she was pregnant, her preparations for a baby girl made her realise a new passion. She spent numerous hours a day online looking at baby clothes. This sparked the idea of starting an online store for baby clothes.

The clouds were as puffs of radiant joy, ready to disperse into the wind and travel the sky. They gracefully floated away until all that remained was the perfect baby blue sky. The nice lady at reception had suggested they take the sky tram to get the full view of Stone Mountain.

While they were waiting in line, they overheard an elderly gentleman say in a Georgia Deep South accent, "If it's not too grey or cloudy, you should be able to see Atlanta from up there".

They handed their tickets over to the chaperone and when everyone had come through the gate, he escorted them to the sky tram.

Reggie and Carmen sat next to each other holding hands while Esther and Malantha sat right opposite holding tourist flyers. The atmosphere was a happy, positive and refreshing one. "Stone mountain is the largest out cropping of granite, monazite, quartz and granodiorite. It rises 825 feet above the surrounding landscape and also extends 8 miles below the earth's surface. This in addition to hiking trails is the main attraction here, but there are many other activities you can take part in." They listened to the guide as he explained the history of the monument while the tram picked up speed. This was their first outing together so it meant a lot. Esther had agreed to come out and explore and she actually looked like she was almost back to her normal self.

They got to a point where downtown Atlanta was visible in the distance. People got their cameras out and started taking pictures and videos. Esther got out her Sony digital camera and started taking videos as well.

She pointed the camera at Reggie and Carmen and said, "Come on you two, say something."

Carmen showed off her four claw solitaire 18 karat white gold ring which she had started to wear again. She was smiling and talking, but it was too loud to hear what exactly she said. Reggie rubbed her bump and Malantha looked on with pure happiness. The people around them joined in and Esther filmed it all.

The guide's voice blurted out something through the loud speakers "hold on tight, we're going to move on now, I hope you enjoyed that. Some folks say that's the best way to see Atlanta.., from a distance." Everyone in tram chuckled and that seemed to be the general mood for the entire tour and day.

Reggie had been having reoccurring dreams of his mother and father. At first he thought they would go away, but it was increasingly bothering him and affecting his sleep. His mother and father would be sat on edge of an old well. Their legs dangled into the water which appeared to be pitch-black.

Reggie would be lying on a bed at the bottom of the well next to Carmen and their baby. Even though they were submerged in water it seemed as if breathing was not a problem. Suddenly a huge viperfish appears from nowhere. Snapping its needle like teeth and hinged lower jaws diving at Reggie, Carmen and the baby as if to swallow them. When it opens its mouth wide Reggie can see bloody faces of Chris, Aleixo, Mr Dean, and others telling him to join him. He notices his father and mother lowering a rope down to him so he can tie Carmen and the baby on it. Before the rope reaches him the viperfish swallows Carmen and the baby then it swims off into the darkness.

Reggie grabs on to the rope and climbs up to the top of the well. He starts to scream out loud because he notices his whole family sitting down facing some Baphomet looking creature sat in a throne. His screams are not heard, he tries to run, but he seems stuck on the spot. The creature focuses its attention on him and he can feel its spirit enter him and that's when he wakes up gasping.

They lived in a neighbourhood were the houses were set on large pieces of property, hidden from the roads by trees, and accessible by long driveways. You would often see squirrels, rabbits and the like crossing the streets. One day on his way driving from work Reggie felt a bump and thought he'd hit something. He stopped the car, looked around and under the car, but didn't see anything. He got back into the car and started to drive off.

"Maybe the animal is stuck under the car", he told himself. He got out again, this time actually going underneath the car to check.

That's when he saw a squirrel lodged in one of the tyres. The squirrel looked like it had a goat's head which immediately scared him. In an instant the creature opened its mouth wide; the gaping mouth was bigger than its body. A laser like beam of light escaped from its mouth straight into Reggie's mouth. His eyes illuminated and the sadistic soul of the evil spirit entered him. Moments after the air snapped and sizzled then it became quiet.

"Are you ok buddy? We were worried because as we drove past we didn't see your legs moving, are you sure you're ok?" the two strangers said while helping Reggie get up on his feet.

"I'm ok, I'm ok thank you. I don't know I thought I hit something", he explained while pointing underneath the car and rubbing his head with the other hand in absolute confusion.

The two strangers inspected the car carefully and couldn't see anything, not a dent, or even any signs of blood.

"Are you sure you hit something buddy? There's nothing there, must have been a long day, be careful and get yourself home."

They got into their car and drove off. Reggie could not understand what happened if at all it had happened. He couldn't get himself to explain to the men what he thought had happened. Apart from a slight headache he felt alright. From there onwards all he thought about was his conversation with Aleixo, he could hear him say, "You can't escape it, they always find you, and it's in your blood."

That evening he got home and went about his usual routine without telling anyone what had happened. During the night when everyone was sleeping he heard a voice in him say, "Simukah Gorah."

It started off as a whisper and he got up and checked if anyone else was awake in the house. It was just him. The voice started to get louder and louder to the point where he couldn't ignore it. When he paid attention he felt something possessing him and giving him incredible strength. Suddenly he started to feel thirsty like a man who'd been stranded on a desert for days. However, the only liquid that could quench the thirst he had was blood.

The end